FINAL WARNING

"Oh, no! Not another note!"

Amanda Hart tore the pale blue envelope off her locker and crumpled it in her hand without opening it. She knew what was inside. This was the fifth note she'd received in the past two weeks. Each note was typed on the same pale blue stationery.

Her best friend, Pepper Larson, raised her eyebrows. "What is it, a love letter?"

"Hardly," Amanda said.

Amanda tore open the top of the envelope and pulled out the thin piece of stationery inside. She read the note and fell back heavily against the wall of the hallway. "This is worse than I thought."

"Let me see." Pepper grabbed the paper from Amanda's hand and gasped as she read its contents. There, in bold type, was printed the warning:

Kill The Story—Or I'll Kill You!

HART AND SOUL #1

KILL THE STORY

JAHNNA N. MALCOLM

BANTAM BOOKS
NEW YORK · TORONTO · LONDON · SYDNEY · AUCKLAND

RL 6, IL age 12 and up

KILL THE STORY
A Bantam Book / May 1990

ISBN 0-553-27969-6

Published simultaneously in the United States and Canada

Bantam Books are published by Bantam Books, a division of Bantam Doubleday Dell Publishing Group, Inc. Its trademark, consisting of the words "Bantam Books" and the portrayal of a rooster, is Registered in U.S. Patent and Trademark Office and in other countries. Marca Registrada. Bantam Books, 666 Fifth Avenue, New York, New York 10103.

PRINTED IN THE UNITED STATES OF AMERICA

OPM   0 9 8 7 6 5 4 3 2 1

For Norma and Charles Beecham

Who have asked for nothing
And given everything.

CHAPTER ONE

O h, no! Not another note!"

Amanda Hart tore the pale blue envelope off her locker and crumpled it in her hand without opening it. She knew what was inside. This was the fifth note she'd received in the past two weeks. Each note was typed on the same pale blue stationery. Each had the same threatening message.

Amanda ran one hand through her thick dark hair and leaned back against the bank of lockers. It was turning out to be a lousy day at Sutter Academy.

The morning had been fabulous, one of those brisk fall days that made San Francisco famous. Just the kind of day Amanda loved best. She'd thrown on her favorite long denim skirt, a crisply starched tuxedo shirt, and looped two leather belts around her trim waist. A black suede jacket completed the outfit.

Slipping out of the house before anyone else had stirred, Amanda had taken a long, glorious ride on her white scooter. At that early hour the mist was still curling in under the Golden Gate Bridge, and the sight lifted her spirits. By the time she arrived at school, Amanda felt ready to take on the world.

Then everything fell apart. First the report she had written for Junior English had completely disappeared from her backpack. Then, at lunchtime, she discovered a flat on her scooter. Finally the envelope with its enclosed warning appeared on her locker.

Amanda closed her eyes and murmured, "How could a Monday start out so great and end up so rotten?"

"Talking to yourself again?" a familiar voice cracked.

Amanda opened her dark green eyes and found herself staring directly into the face of her best friend, Pepper Larson.

"That's a bad habit," the curly-topped redhead said. She stood with her hands on her hips, an amused grin on her face. Pepper had on her usual uniform of green khaki pants, Oxford cloth shirt and oversize cotton vest. Around her neck hung her ever present 35mm Nikon camera. As the lone photographer for the *Sutter Spectator*, her motto was "Be prepared!" If anything of significance happened at Sutter Academy, Pepper Larson was ready to record it on film.

"Pepper?" Amanda cocked her head to look at her friend. "Have you ever had one of those days when you think a brick could fall on your head or you might get hit by a car?"

"That bad?"

"That bad." Amanda started to show Pepper the note but suddenly thought better of it. The main corridor was crowded with students bustling to their final class of the day. Amanda shoved the note into the pocket of her jacket and looped her arm through Pepper's. "I can't talk now. I'll tell you when we get to Journalism, okay?"

The two friends moved down the hall of the main building at Sutter Academy. Several guys making their way to class were tossing a football back and forth. One of them, Randy Stafford, collided with Pepper.

"Watch where you're walking, you big lug!" she shouted. "There *are* other students at this school."

Randy, a tall, muscular senior, stared down at Pepper, who stood all of five feet two inches in height, and chuckled. "Sorry, pip-squeak, I didn't see you down there."

"Pip-squeak!" Pepper watched him jog off to join his buddies and grumbled, "Wait till I reach my full height. That moose'll never know what hit him."

Amanda tried to force a smile, but she couldn't stop thinking about the note.

Pepper pushed her round wire-rim glasses up on her nose and peered at Amanda carefully. "Boy, you *must* be having a bad day. I haven't seen that Hart killer smile once."

"What killer smile?" Amanda asked.

"The one that causes the boys at Sutter to turn into puppy dogs and the girls into hissing cats."

"Oh, Pepper, you're exaggerating," Amanda said, giving her friend a good-natured shove. "As usual."

The two girls exited into the open-air garden that lay between the east and west wings of the academy. Beautiful plants and trees lined the red-tiled patio. At the center of the garden sat a three-tiered marble fountain surrounded by curved granite benches. The fountain had been there since the mansion had been converted into a school, sixty years before.

The fountain matched the Spanish-style architecture of the school. The patio was called the Hub because at some point during each day every student passed through there.

"Listen, Pepper, before, at my locker I—"

"Amanda! Amanda Hart! I need to talk to you."

Amanda and Pepper frowned as a plump boy with dark hair and dark-framed glasses hurried across the patio toward them.

"Oh, great!" Pepper muttered. "It's Jason Stuart, the Greaseman."

Jason had long, limp black hair that he smeared with gel to keep it in place. His efforts at style earned him his nickname.

"I need to talk to you," Jason huffed when he reached the girls. "About the paper."

"Journalism is next hour," Pepper cut in. "Can't it wait?"

"No, it cannot," he replied curtly.

"What's the matter, Jase?" Amanda asked, suppressing a sigh.

He placed his briefcase on the nearest stone bench and withdrew a stack of papers. "I worked on this article for a solid month. It's well researched, informative, and newsworthy. Just the kind of material the *Spectator* needs. Now I find out it's going to be bumped from this issue."

"That's right." Amanda nodded. "I'm sorry about that, but Mr. Mooney and I decided to use it next issue instead."

"So I hear." Jason returned the sheaf of papers to his briefcase and snapped the lid shut. "He told me a special version of *HartBeat* was to take its place."

HartBeat was Amanda's newspaper column and her pride and joy. As editor in chief of the *Sutter Spectator,* she spent much of her time editing and revising other people's writing. *HartBeat* gave her the chance to explore and express her own thoughts and feelings. Occasionally she'd used the column to do an in-depth study on school activities, usually finding an interesting angle for her reporting.

"So what is it you want, Jason?" Amanda asked.

"I want you to withdraw your column from the issue."

"Jason, I can't do that," Amanda protested. "It's the second installment in a three-part series."

"On sororities at Sutter." His lips curled into a sneer. "Stupid sororities. As if anyone cared."

"I guess some people do," Amanda replied evenly.

"Sutter has three of them, and over seventy people belong. That's almost a third of the student body."

"Hey, Jase," Pepper cut in, squinting up at him, "what's your article about, anyway?"

"The Science Fair," he replied. "It chronicles my project and the process I have gone through getting to the finals."

Pepper burst out laughing and Amanda nudged her with her elbow. Jason Stuart was pompous and abrasive, and he totally lacked a sense of humor. However, he was a good writer, particularly on technical subjects. Amanda didn't want to lose a capable writer just by being insensitive.

"Look, Jason, we've already finished the layout for this week's issue. In fact, we're sending it to the printer's this afternoon."

"I can't believe you'd *do* this to me!" the boy cried out. He sounded as if he were in pain. Amanda stared at him in surprise. Talk about a case of wounded pride!

"How about this?" Amanda suggested, putting her hand on his arm to reassure him. "I'll give your article priority in the next issue. Page One. Okay?"

Usually Jason turned to jelly around her, but not today.

"Don't patronize me!" he shouted, jerking his arm away. "You don't understand. That article has *got* to be in this week's issue or . . . or else!"

Amanda responded calmly. "Don't you think you're overreacting to this a little?"

He shook his head. "This could mean the difference between a full scholarship to Stanford and being stuck going to City College." His voice got more whiny. "The deadline for submitting published work is next week. It *has* to be in this issue, or it won't be accepted."

"Jase, if this was so important," Pepper asked, "why didn't you say something about it before?"

"When I found out about the deadline, the article was already scheduled to go into this issue. I thought I was fine." He looked darkly at Amanda. "Then I got stabbed in the back by an egomaniacal editor in chief."

Amanda took a deep breath and struggled to contain the urge to tell Jason where to get off. "Why not submit the article on the Dungeons and Dragons Club you wrote for the first fall issue? It's already been published and I thought it was really good."

"No!" Jason was adamant. "I refuse to be pushed around like this. It has to be this article, or nothing!"

"Who's pushing who, you jerk?" Pepper demanded angrily. "You can't talk to Amanda like that!"

"Relax, Pep," Amanda said, smiling at her friend's fierce loyalty. "Look, Jason, I'm sorry about what's happened. I can't promise anything, but I'll see what I can do to help you out."

"You do that," he shot back, "or you can just find yourself another reporter!" He snatched up his briefcase and stormed off across the Hub.

"What a slime!" Pepper muttered. "He sure loses my vote for Mr. Congeniality."

"And mine," Amanda said, staring after him. "I've never seen Jason act like that before."

Pepper looked at her friend closely. "Amanda, you

aren't going to put his article in the paper, are you? After the way he just treated you?"

"I don't know," Amanda replied with a sigh. "Maybe we can add an extra page, or put in an insert, or something."

"Forget it. He's just being a big baby," Pepper declared. "You can't worry about him."

But Amanda was worrying. She had seen a look in Jason's eyes that frightened her. He looked desperate. She thought of the note in her purse and reminded herself to be on guard.

"Mandy!" A pretty blond placed a manicured hand on Amanda's arm. Her nails were painted a blushing pink that matched the color of her lipstick exactly. "I've been looking for you for days."

"Hi, Janis." Amanda smiled at the blue-eyed beauty beside her. "You look terrific. As usual."

Janis accepted the compliment with a pleased nod. Along with perfectly cut shoulder-length hair and a pert turned-up nose, Janis Stevens had a slim figure that made the most of the clothes she wore. Today she wore a pale blue angora sweater with a lace collar. Peeking out of the neckline was a set of pearls that Amanda knew had to be real.

"Listen, I just wanted to compliment you on your article on Sutter's sororities," Janis said. "All of the girls in Entre Nous have been talking about it, ever since it came out last week."

"One yea, and one nay," Pepper whispered to Amanda.

"I'm glad you liked it," Amanda said. "It's been kind

of fun finding out about Sutter's history and traditions."

Amanda had spent several weeks interviewing past and present members of the three sororities and poring over old yearbooks. It had given her a chance to find out about her school and meet a lot of people in the bargain.

"Tradition is so important to a Sutter sorority," Janis said solemnly.

Amanda smiled. "Entre Nous certainly does seem to have the lock on that."

"My great-grandmother was one of the founding members here at Sutter," Janis said proudly. "My grandmother and mother both followed in her footsteps. And I'm trying my best to live up to their expectations."

"Seems like you've already surpassed them," Pepper remarked. "You're the first in your family to become president, right?"

Janis nodded and then glanced at her gold wristwatch. "Excuse me, but I'd better run. Madame Gautier hates it when I'm late for French."

"It was good talking to you," Amanda said.

"Oh, one other thing." Janis put one finger to her lips. "I noticed that it's to be a three-part series. What more is there to say? I mean, won't the student body get bored?"

"I don't think so," Amanda replied. "Part Two is written from a pledge's point of view. I think a lot of the freshman and sophomore girls will be interested in that."

"Not any of the girls I know," another voice cut in. Whitney Powell, president of a rival sorority, Delta Psi, stood with her arms folded across her chest. She glared at Amanda angrily.

"Why, hello, Whitney," Pepper cooed from behind Amanda's shoulder. "What a *pleasant* surprise!" She and Whitney had known each other since grade school and had loathed each other from the start. "Something on your mind?"

"You bet there is!" Whitney shook her long mane of auburn hair, and all of the jewelry she wore flashed in the afternoon light. Three gold hoops dangled from her left ear, gold and silver bracelets jangled from her wrists, and the gold belt on her black leather miniskirt gleamed as she adjusted it.

"Our clubs are service organizations that do a lot for this school," Whitney declared in a strident voice that echoed around the Hub.

"I never said they didn't," Amanda replied.

Whitney narrowed her dark eyes. "No, but you hinted at it by putting so much emphasis on parties and sorority social life."

"If that emphasis is there, it's because the people I interviewed seemed to think it was important and wanted to talk about it."

"Who do you think you are, *60 Minutes*?" Whitney said sarcastically. "Trying to find out the deep, dark secrets at Sutter? Well, there are none!"

"Whoa! Wait a minute." Amanda held up one hand. "Calm down, Whitney."

"I am very upset."

"I can see that," Amanda replied. "But I'm not sure what it is that you're afraid of."

"Afraid? Who said I was afraid?"

Amanda shrugged. "Well, I wrote a pretty straightforward article on all of the sororities, not just Delta Psi."

"Yeah, but you hit the Delts the hardest."

"How?"

"By labeling us the party sorority, that's how."

"Well, aren't you?" Amanda couldn't help smiling. Every Friday and Saturday night a party was usually being thrown somewhere by one of the Delts, the more outlandish and extravagant, the better.

"That is completely beside the point," Whitney huffed. "I think you're just upset because we didn't invite you to join when you came to Sutter last year. Now you're trying to tear us all down."

"That's not true," Amanda snapped back. She had never really joined clubs anywhere she had lived. It just wasn't her style. But from the look on Whitney's face, she knew she'd never be able to convince her of that.

As the few remaining students on the Hub turned to stare, Amanda felt her cheeks start to heat up. Whitney took advantage of Amanda's silence to shout, "You can't just march in here and start changing things. We'll make sure you're stopped."

The loud chime sounded through the speakers, and Whitney turned on her heel and stomped off to her next class.

"Saved by the bell," Amanda murmured. She stood

watching the door where Whitney had disappeared and shook her head. "I feel like I've been hit by a tornado."

"You have." Pepper grabbed her by the elbow and guided her down the path toward the building where Journalism was held. "And Whitney can be fierce, especially when she thinks you're trying to steal her guy."

"What are you talking about?"

"Chip Langsdale, football hero," Pepper replied. "The guy who was always flirting with you in Mr. Cunningham's class."

"But Pepper, that was last June, when I first got here," Amanda exclaimed. She had spoken with Chip once or twice before class, and once they'd exchanged some notes on homework. She remembered him as being fairly nice to her.

"Whitney is like an elephant," Pepper chuckled. "She never forgets."

Amanda's head was spinning as they walked up the shaded path toward the Journalism classroom. First there had been her ugly encounter with Jason. Fortunately, Janis had been sweet, but Whitney more than made up for her. Finally, there was that threatening note weighing heavily in her pocket.

"Pepper," Amanda said, pulling her friend to the side of the Journalism building. "There's one more thing." She pulled the blue envelope out of her pocket. "I found this taped to my locker."

"Oh?" Pepper wiggled her eyebrows. "What is it, a love letter?"

"Hardly," Amanda said, thinking of the four other notes she'd received.

"Go on, open it," Pepper demanded. "Before I do."

Amanda tore open the top of the envelope and pulled out the thin piece of stationery inside. She read the note and fell back heavily against the wall of the building. "This is worse than I thought."

"Let me see." Pepper grabbed the paper from Amanda's hand and gasped as she read its contents. There, in bold type, was printed the warning:

Kill the Story—or I'll Kill You!

CHAPTER TWO

I 'm going to the headmistress," Pepper declared. "Miss Wilson should know about this."

Amanda grabbed her friend by the arm. "Don't you dare! That would be the end of the newspaper."

When Amanda had arrived at Sutter, the newspaper was on its last legs. The budget had been whittled down to almost nothing, and only Pepper and one or two other students were interested in keeping it alive. Amanda had coaxed Miss Wilson into letting them continue publishing.

"Look, Mandy, this note is serious and has nothing to do with the paper."

"It has everything to do with it," Amanda said. "This would be the perfect excuse for Miss Wilson to shut

the *Spectator* down and put the budget into something else." Her voice dropped to a whisper. "Please,
Pep, this is really important to me."

As a child, Amanda had changed schools as often as
every two years. Her parents, Del and Dinah Hart,
were a famous team of photojournalists who roamed
the globe following stories. Working on school newspapers had always been Amanda's way of quickly fit-
ting into the life of her new schools. It had often been
the only thing she could count on in an uncertain life.

"Okay, I'll keep my mouth shut." Pepper pushed
her glasses up on her nose and studied her friend's
face. "But what are you going to do about the note?"

Amanda shrugged. "Find out who's writing them."

"*Them?*" Pepper's eyes were wide as saucers. "What
do you mean, *them?* You mean, you've gotten more
than one of these?"

Amanda nodded. "This is the fifth one. It is also the
most vicious. The others just said 'kill the story.'"

Pepper shook her head. "I don't like this. I don't
like it one bit."

"Look, I'm not exactly thrilled by it myself."
Amanda looped her arm over Pepper's shoulder.
"We'll just do some detective work and find out who's
behind this."

She threw open the door to the Journalism room
and was immediately assaulted by a heavy, musty
smell. The little building had originally been the car-
riage house of the old estate. It sat right in the alley
running behind the school grounds. For years, the

school had used it to store garden supplies, and once the science class had kept chickens there. It was just in the last year that the building had been converted into the Journalism classroom. Amanda and Pepper liked to call it the Coop.

A couple of long tables sat in the center of the room. On the right wall was a table with an overhead lamp for doing layouts and pasteup. An old-fashioned typewriter perched on top of a rusty filing cabinet.

Against the far wall was the paper's lone computer and printer. A solitary figure sat huddled over the keyboard, his fingers clicking away as words and figures moved about the illuminated screen.

"It's my favorite cousin," Amanda called out gaily. She added to Pepper under her breath, "At least I can be pretty sure Josh won't bite my head off."

Josh Pickering turned in his chair and gave Amanda a startled look. He'd been concentrating so hard that he hadn't heard them come in. When the sandy-haired freshman recognized his cousin, his freckled face broke into a crooked grin.

"Mandy! I'm glad you're here. I've almost finished keying in all the formatting data. We can get this stuff to the printer's by . . ." He checked the large black diver's watch on his thin forearm. "Four, at the latest."

"Thanks, Josh," Amanda said. "I knew I could count on you."

Ever since she'd moved to San Francisco, her cousin had always been there for her. Amanda's family had decided it was best that she spend her final years of high school in one spot. So the previous June,

Amanda had come to live with her Aunt Jane and Uncle Silas Pickering. Even though her cousin Josh was almost three years younger, they'd become fast friends.

Amanda hung her backpack on the nearest chair and crossed the room to her cousin. "Where's everybody?"

"Mr. Mooney spilled coffee on his tie and went off to Main Hall to find something to remove it."

Amanda laughed. "Sounds typical."

Pepper agreed. "He'll probably get lost and we won't see him for the rest of the hour."

Mr. Mooney was the Spanish teacher at Sutter. Out of the goodness of his heart, he had volunteered to be the faculty advisor for the *Sutter Spectator*. He knew absolutely nothing about journalism and usually spent the hour chatting with the students. Everyone was fond of him but teased him unmercifully about his chronic absentmindedness.

"Dee Hardwick is out sick this week," Josh added. "And Jason Stuart stomped in here muttering something about sororities, and warped priorities, and then stomped out again."

Amanda nodded ruefully. "I doubt if he'll be back again today. He's pretty upset. I bumped his article on the Science Fair from this issue."

"He's acting like an idiot, Amanda," Pepper said. "Forget him." She hopped up onto one of the counters and whispered loudly to Josh, "Your cousin is feeling responsible for everybody's problems again. Tell her to stop it."

"Mandy's like that." Josh turned an adoring smile in Amanda's direction. "That's the best part about her."

"Well, if she's not careful, she's going to get her feelings—not to mention her body—*hurt*." Pepper folded her arms and ordered, "Tell Josh about the note."

Amanda tried to silence Pepper with a warning look, but her friend was adamant. "He should know. And maybe he can help us figure out who's behind it."

Amanda dug into her jacket and reluctantly handed her cousin the note. "I've been getting these ever since the last issue of the *Spectator* came out. I think they're just a silly prank—"

"I think they're a lot more serious than that," Pepper cut in. "And they all must be related to that one story about the sororities. It's the only article you did."

Josh studied the note with a frown. "I think you should look carefully at the article you wrote to see which sorority might have been upset by it," he suggested. "Then maybe you could see who has stationery like this. It looks pretty fancy." He held the stationery up to the light. "Look at the watermark."

The two girls leaned over and examined the slip of paper. An elegant figure of a prancing horse was visible on the lower corner of the note.

"Atta boy, Josh!" Pepper clapped her hands together. "I knew the computer whiz might have some ideas."

Amanda opened the one closet that held last week's issue and gasped. "You guys better come look at this."

The leftover issues of the previous edition were

stacked on the floor as usual, but the issue lying on top had been opened to Amanda's column. Mr. Mooney's letter opener, an ornate one with a brass handle, stood on end. It had been stabbed through Amanda's name.

Josh and Pepper stared at the closet in horrified silence. "This is major serious," Pepper moaned.

"Hey! What have you got in the closet?" a voice called from the door. Pepper, Amanda, and Josh spun around so hard they fell into each other.

Amanda stammered, "We were just noticing that we were, uh, running short of paper."

Brad Elliot, a short, muscular guy, sauntered over to join them. "You call that serious?"

Pepper jumped in front of him. "It is, when you're trying to write a newspaper."

"Oh, right." Brad nodded pleasantly. He perched on the corner of the pasteup table and smiled at Amanda.

Brad Elliot was the kind of guy used to having girls fall all over him. He was handsome, friendly, and president of the student council. Amanda wondered why she didn't find him attractive. In his tan chinos, loafers, striped rep tie, and blue blazer, Brad looked like an ad for a men's fashion magazine.

". . . which is why I need to ask this favor of you," Brad was saying as he fixed his dazzling smile on her. With a start Amanda realized she hadn't heard a word he'd been saying. She knit her brow in confusion and he added, "Look, if you put the announcement about the Fall Fest in this week's issue, I'll owe you one."

"But, Brad, the layout's already done and ready to

go to the printer's," Amanda said. "The deadline for school activities submissions was last week."

"I explained why I missed it," he said patiently. Brad took both of her hands in his and added, "Look, the dance is Friday. The students need to know about it so they can buy tickets. Do me this one little favor and maybe, just maybe, I'll be your date for the dance." He gave her a quick wink.

Amanda remembered instantly why she didn't care for Brad. He was a complete egotist. She withdrew her hands and said, "Look, Brad, I'll think about it."

"About what? The announcement, or the date?" He leaned forward and leered. "Or both?"

Amanda pushed her hair off her forehead and sighed. "The announcement, Brad. I'll see what I can do."

Brad hopped off the table and leaned over to whisper into Josh's ear. "Your cousin is beautiful, but sometimes she can be a total iceberg. Get her to warm up for me, will you?"

Josh didn't answer but stared hard at the computer screen. The tips of his ears turned bright pink.

Amanda could see that Brad had embarrassed Josh, and that made her furious. She grabbed Brad's elbow and ushered him to the door. "You may have time to waste, but we have a paper to put out. So *adios, amigo!*"

"Wait a minute, Mandy," the boy protested. Amanda pushed him firmly out the door, then slammed it shut. "So much for him."

Without another word she marched over to the

closet, removed the letter opener from the stack of newspapers, and, taking one of the papers, spread it out on top of the long wooden table.

"Let's get down to business. As I see it, most of the sorority article was pretty formal. I mean, the whole first half covered the history of sororities here at Sutter, tradition, how much they mean to the alumnae, and all of that."

"Yeah." Pepper nodded. "Pretty boring stuff."

Amanda raised an eyebrow in protest and Pepper added quickly, "You know what I mean."

"The only thing I see that could possibly have upset someone might have been where I described a few of the pranks they've played." She shrugged. "But that was all pretty harmless stuff."

Pepper leaned in and peered over her shoulder. "The blackballing procedures are something these clubs probably don't want people to know about."

"Yeah, but the girls all talk about them," Amanda countered. "It's common knowledge around the school. I don't think that's it, either."

"Mentioning those wild Delta parties sure upset Whitney," Pepper reminded her friend.

"True. But enough to make her send threatening notes?"

Pepper shook her head and stared at the article. "It just doesn't make any sense."

"There's one thing you haven't discussed," Josh offered.

"What's that?" Pepper asked.

He pointed at the last line of the article. Amanda

read out loud, "First of three parts, to be continued next issue."

"You mean, they're not afraid of what's in this article," Pepper exclaimed, "but what might be in the next one?"

Josh nodded. "Exactly. The pledge's point of view."

"Hey, that could be it." Amanda gave her cousin a hug. "Josh, you are so smart!" The tips of his ears turned red again, but this time from pleasure.

Pepper slapped the table decisively. "Then that settles it."

"What do you mean?"

"I don't think you should run the next article," Pepper explained. "If it's got something in it that's causing all this trouble, we'll have Josh remove it right now. You can substitute Brad's dumb dance announcement." She grimaced and added, "Or Jason's Science Fair masterpiece."

"You mean, kill the story," Amanda said.

"Right."

"Never!" Amanda declared and put her hands on her hips. "I will not be intimidated by anonymous threats."

"Threats that say, 'I'll kill you' are pretty scary," Pepper argued. "The least you can do is take a few precautions, until we figure out who's writing these notes."

Josh nodded his agreement. "Pepper is right. I think you should take her with you when you drive to the printer's."

"We'll have to take your car, Pepper," Amanda said. "My scooter's got a flat."

"When did that happen?" Josh asked. "It was fine this morning."

"I know. But when I went to the parking lot at lunchtime, the tire was as flat as a pancake."

Pepper and Josh exchanged looks. "Sounds awfully coincidental, if you ask me," Pepper said.

"Oh, come on," Amanda scoffed, "let's not get carried away here."

"If someone could get into the Journalism building and stab a stack of newsprint," Josh reminded her, "they could certainly slash a tire."

"Who said it was slashed?"

"I'll bet you ten dollars it was," Pepper said.

Amanda didn't take her up on it. She was frankly becoming a little worried herself. "Everything is getting so odd. I wonder if the same person who flattened my tire also stole my report?"

"You didn't tell me about that," Pepper chastised her.

"I thought I'd lost it. But now it all seems to fit together."

"That really does it," Pepper said. "I'm driving the stuff to the printer's myself."

"No way!" Amanda shook her head. "It looks like they don't want the article to get to the printer's. I'm afraid they'll try and stop any one of us if we're seen delivering it."

"Then what do you suggest? We hide here until dark, then sneak over and slide it under the printer's door?"

"The thought had crossed my mind," Amanda replied with a grin.

"How about a messenger service?" Josh suggested. "That way, no one would see any of us leave."

Pepper raced for the yellow pages buried in the closet. "What should I look for?" she asked as she thumbed through the pages. "Some sort of taxi company?"

"No, those bicycle services," Josh replied. "I think they're cool."

"Sure they are," Amanda retorted, "weaving in and out of traffic like maniacs, scaring pedestrians half to death. *Real* cool."

"I like them." Josh shrugged. "They can go where cars can't."

"He's got a point," Pepper added. "I don't think anyone would be looking for a cyclist to be delivering our galleys, do you?"

"Okay." Amanda ran her hand up the long column of names, muttering, "Let's see . . . Speedy, Mercury, Lightning, Fleet Street . . ." She stopped and chuckled softly. "It's perfect."

"What *is?*" Pepper blinked at her from behind her glasses.

"Fleet Street is where the great newspapers in London were headquartered years ago. It's famous all over the world. We're a newspaper, Mom and Dad are in London right now working on a story, so it must be good luck."

"That's good enough for me." Pepper moved to the desk and pulled out the phone that was kept in the bottom drawer. "Give me the number and I'll have them send a guy right over. Preferably a hunk who likes redheaded girls with glasses."

Amanda grinned at her friend. "The number is easy. Just dial FLEET-ST."

CHAPTER THREE

The first thing Amanda noticed about him when she pulled open the door were his piercing blue eyes. Clear, blue eyes framed in thick, dark lashes. *How could a boy have such long lashes?* she wondered.

"Did you call Fleet Street?" His voice was low and husky.

"Yes." Only her lips moved. Amanda couldn't stop staring.

His eyes met hers in a steady gaze. He was waiting for her to make the next move.

Amanda stepped backward to let him into the room and her foot caught on the loose strap of her backpack. She stumbled, taking the chair it was hanging on and a sheaf of papers with her, and hit the floor with a loud thud.

"Hey, are you okay?" The dark-haired boy held out his hand to help her up. "That was some trick you just did. Do you think you could do it again?"

"Not in a million years." Amanda felt the blood rush to her face. She giggled a little too loudly. "Today just isn't my day."

He pulled her to her feet, and her face was inches from his. Once again their eyes locked. One half of Amanda's mind told her to get a hold of herself and stop acting so silly. The other noticed the slight cleft in his chin and the fact that he was slightly taller than she was, perhaps a shade under six feet. She didn't pull away.

"Hey, is this a private party?" Pepper asked, sticking her face in between them. "Or can anyone join?"

Amanda stepped back quickly and spun in a circle. "Uh, let's see. We called you because we need to have something delivered to the printer's this afternoon." Amanda ran her hand through her hair. "If I could just remember where we put it."

"Do you always have this effect on girls?" Pepper asked the stranger, fluttering her lashes at him.

His lips parted in an amused grin, and Amanda thought she would melt through the floor. He was even more attractive when he smiled.

"I hardly see any girls in my line of business." He leaned easily against the table. His jeans were faded with age and had a hole in the right knee. They fit him like a second skin. A white T-shirt peeked out of the top of his worn leather jacket, and he had a pen tucked behind one ear. "Most of the deliveries I make are to the financial district. You know, older secretaries, guys in pin-striped monkey suits." He grinned and added, "Real live wires."

"I guess you don't get too many calls from high schools." Amanda forced her voice to sound casual.

"No." He shook his head, and a lock of dark hair fell over one eye. "This is a first."

"Boy, you're fast," Pepper said. "I mean, we called you less than fifteen minutes ago."

He stuck his hands in his pockets and shrugged. "Speed's the name of the game at Fleet Street."

Amanda was still shuffling through the papers on her desk and checking under books, but her attention remained focused on the dark-haired boy.

"Mandy, are you looking for the disks?" Josh asked curiously.

Amanda stood up straight and pushed her hair off her face. "Why, yes I am, Josh. Do you have them?"

"Of course he has them," Pepper said, drily. "He's the only one of us who runs the computer. Who else would have them?"

Sometimes having Pepper as a best friend could be a trial. This was one of those times. Amanda shot her a withering look.

"Here they are." Josh held up two disks.

Mick sauntered over to Josh's computer table. "Nice rig. What are your specs?"

Josh's eyes lit up. "It's your basic PC frame, with a turbo booster that kicks it up to four megs of RAM."

"What kind of language is that?" Pepper crossed her eyes at Amanda. "Sounds like squid talk to me."

Amanda didn't reply. She was watching her cousin in amazement. Josh, who was usually shy around anyone outside the family, was chattering away a mile a minute, explaining in detail every aspect of his computer system. The dark-haired messenger leaned forward, paying close attention to what the younger boy said. Amanda was amazed at how completely this stranger had captivated her cousin.

"I key in the layouts on the PC," Josh said, "then I dump them down to a single three-and-a-half-inch floppy. Oops!" The slender rectangle of plastic slipped out of his hand and flew in the air.

With one hand, the boy snatched it out of the air. His movement was so quick that it hardly seemed to have happened at all.

"Wow!" Josh shook his head, definitely impressed. "That was fast."

"It's all in the reflexes." Then, as if to demonstrate, the boy flipped the disk in the air behind his back and caught it with the other hand without looking. "See? Nothing to it."

Josh and Pepper applauded, and the boy gave them a mock bow. When he stood up he faced Josh, holding out his upturned palm. "The name's Mickey Soul."

Josh slapped his hand. "Josh Pickering." The boys

gave each other a high five, then turned to face the girls.

Pepper raised her camera and snapped their picture. Then she lowered the Nikon and smiled her most alluring smile. "I'm Pepper Larson, the staff photographer."

"And I'm Amanda Hart," Amanda said, trying to regain her composure. "Editor in chief of the *Sutter Spectator*."

"So you're the boss?" Mickey Soul raised his hand, and for one awful moment Amanda was afraid she would have to go through the whole high and low five routine that she never could figure out and always made her feel so uncool when she tried it. But her fears were quickly put to rest.

Mick touched his forehead in a quick salute and said, "Pepper. Amanda. My pleasure." Mick pulled out a form and offered Amanda the pen from behind his ear. "I need your name and seven digits."

Amanda shook her head in confusion.

Mick grinned. "Your phone number, for the records." He leaned over her shoulder and pointed to the line she was to write on. "And the destination of the delivery here."

Mick was so close to her face that she could almost feel the heat radiating from his skin. He smelled good, like fresh, clean soap. A voice inside Amanda ordered her to pay attention. *You have more important things to worry about*, she told herself. *Like those notes, and getting this paper out on time*.

Amanda forced herself to sound businesslike. "If

you could get it to the printer's before four, that would be great." She went to her backpack, which was still entangled with the chair. Pulling out her billfold, she paid him the delivery fee. "Thanks."

"Anytime." He pulled a black beret out of his hip pocket and placed it on his head.

Pepper, Josh, and Amanda watched as Mick threw open the door and strolled out into the afternoon light. His bike leaned against the old garden wall by the alley. It was a faded blue ten-speed that had definitely seen better days. Bits of black electrical tape were wound around the rusted handlebars. Over the back fender hung a gray canvas bag with faded handmade lettering stenciled on it that read, *FLEET STREET*.

Amanda and Pepper glanced at each other, shocked at the bike's dilapidated appearance. Without turning around, Mickey Soul declared, "Never judge a book by its cover." With that, he hopped onto the seat and, popping a wheelie, spun the front wheel around in circles. Then, in a spray of gravel, he disappeared down the alley.

"He's gone." Amanda couldn't hide the disappointment in her voice. Like a character in a romantic novel, a dark, handsome stranger had walked into her life—and right back out of it.

"He may be gone," Pepper replied, "but I have his picture. I can look at those blue eyes and that neat little cleft in his chin as often as I like."

Amanda realized that Mickey Soul had had the same effect on her best friend.

"Hey," Pepper said, her face brightening. "Maybe we can always have Fleet Street deliver our disks to the printer. That way we'd see him at least once a week."

"But Fleet Street could be a huge outfit," Josh pointed out. "We might not always get Mick."

"We'll just ask for him." Pepper pushed her glasses up on her nose. "Listen, that's the first interesting guy I've seen since school started. I'm not letting him get away."

"Oh, Pepper, you're just attracted to him 'cause he wasn't wearing a tie," Amanda teased. "I think you go for guys with holes in their clothes."

"Don't lecture me, Miss Hart." Pepper wagged her finger at Amanda. "I saw the way you fell for him. Literally." She shook her red curls in mock disgust. "Tripping over the chair, then giggling like a goon. Really!"

"I did not!" Amanda shouted indignantly.

"You did too!" Pepper retorted.

"Well . . . Well . . ." Amanda stomped around the room, trying to think of a clever comeback. Finally she slammed the door of the closet and yelled, "You try having your life threatened and see if you don't act a little stupid."

Amanda's sudden temper tantrum made Pepper and Josh burst out laughing. Pepper sang out, "Ooh, I think we've found your cousin's weak spot, Josh."

Amanda suddenly felt absurd for getting so angry. She put her hands on her hips and glared at her companions. "You two are impossible." She threw her hands in the air. "Okay, so I thought he was attractive. Who wouldn't? But that doesn't mean I'm going to be calling Fleet Street every few minutes."

"Well, if we don't call Fleet Street," Pepper said, "who should we call?"

"A doctor!" a male voice answered from the doorway. "I've been mugged."

Mick Soul leaned against the doorsill, trying to catch his breath. The collar of his jacket was torn. His face and clothes were smeared in dirt, and a small stream of blood dripped from the corner of his mouth.

"What happened?" Pepper shrieked. "You look awful!"

"It's nothing compared to how I feel." Mick limped into the room and slumped down in the nearest chair.

Josh headed out the door.

"*Where* are you going?" Amanda yelled.

"To see which way the muggers went," he replied.

"Don't you dare!" she commanded. "Those thugs might still be out there. Do you want to wind up like him?"

She gestured at Mick, who was feeling his head gingerly with his hand. Blood trickled down his face from another cut on his forehead. The hole in his jeans now covered most of his leg, which was smeared with gravel and blood.

"She's right, champ," Mick murmured. He smiled at Josh and added, "But thanks for trying."

Amanda raced to Mr. Mooney's desk and grabbed the first aid kit from out of the middle drawer. All that remained in the dusty white metal box was a brown bottle of hydrogen peroxide and a roll of gauze. She grabbed a pair of scissors and tried to cut it into small squares. "Are you okay?" she asked Mick. "Is anything broken?"

Mick felt his face with his fingers and winced. "Maybe my nose. But it's my wheels I'm worried about. They did a major trash job on my bike."

"What about the disks?" Amanda asked as she patted the cut on his forehead with the peroxide. "Are they still on your bike?"

"Are you kidding?" Mick winced, pushing her hand away from his forehead. "That's why they jumped me. They wanted the disks. What was on them, anyway?"

"Our entire next week's issue of the *Spectator.*"

"A likely story," Mick muttered.

Amanda patted the cut on his forehead once more. "I'm not kidding. That's all it was."

Pepper, who had been trying to wipe off the gravel embedded in his knee, asked, "Did you see who did this?"

"Yeah, I saw them." He grimaced in pain. "It was a gang of about ten. And they meant business." Mick leaned forward in his chair and added, "But here's the really weird part. It was a gang of girls."

CHAPTER FOUR

I don't see a sign of them anywhere," Pepper called from the parking lot. "How about you guys?"

Josh and Amanda stood by the front gate, scanning the street in front of Sutter Academy. Amanda cupped her hands around her mouth. "Broadway and Fillmore are deserted."

"What'd you expect?" Mick limped up to join them, pushing his ten-speed along with one hand. The battered bicycle rattled and clanked on the gravel beside him. "They were out of the alley and across the street before I knew what hit me."

"Then how did you know they were girls?" Amanda asked.

"I watched them run into the park."

Amanda arched her eyebrow. "So?"

A half-smile flickered across his lips. "Let's just say girls move differently than guys."

Amanda felt her face flush and she quickly changed the subject. "Well, great. Now the disks are gone and we'll miss the deadline for the paper. Whoever wanted to prevent the next issue from coming out has succeeded."

"Mandy, you're forgetting that I made backups," Josh reassured her. "I'll go get them."

"I'm going to Main Hall," Pepper said, running down the hill toward the front of the school. "I want to check on a few things."

"Well, I'm glad to hear it's not a complete loss." Amanda clapped her hands together and turned to face Mick. "You should have just enough time to get to the printer's by four o'clock."

"Whoa, wait a minute!" Mick held up one hand. "Aren't you forgetting something?"

She looked at him, not comprehending.

"I have just been mugged. I think we need to deal with that."

"I did the best I could with that old first aid kit," Amanda replied, squinting at his forehead. "The bleeding seems to have stopped. You can still ride, can't you?"

"Of course, I can still ride," Mick said impatiently. "But let's get something straight here. I am not going *anywhere* without hazard pay."

"Hazard pay?" Amanda repeated.

"Yeah." He pulled their agreement out of his pocket

and held it out toward her. "It's twice the amount, or no go."

"But—but that's not fair," Amanda sputtered. "We agreed on the money already."

"But you didn't warn me that this job was dangerous."

"How could I know?" Amanda could feel her temper starting to rise. "A couple of girls push over your—bike, and you want to blame me."

"Hey, what are you calling a *bike?*" Mick imitated the scornful way she'd said it. "This bike is my livelihood. For your information, these wheels have covered San Francisco more times than you will in your entire lifetime. And while we're on the subject of my *bike*, I'd like the money to get it fixed."

"What?" Amanda exclaimed. "You've got to be kidding." She narrowed her eyes at him. "Is this some kind of a scam you pull? Fake a mugging, then demand more money?"

Mick laughed out loud. "Boy, you are really something! What kind of a person do you think I am, anyway?"

"I don't know," Amanda snapped. "You tell me."

"I'm a businessman, plain and simple," Mick shot back. "I've suffered damages, through no fault of my own, and I think I have a right to be paid for them."

He stared at Amanda, waiting for her to respond. She said nothing. Finally he burst out exasperatedly, "For crying out loud, my bike's a wreck. Look at it!"

"How can you tell it's broken?" Amanda asked sarcastically. "It looks the same to me." She walked around it, pointing as she spoke. "Same rusted handlebars, same peeling paint job—and this *attractive* decoration of shredded black tape has lost none of its eye-catching appeal."

"Very funny." Mick picked up the front end of the ten-speed and spun the wheel with his hand. It had a bad wobble. "You'll notice the frame is bent completely out of alignment. It's almost unusable." He leaned his bike against a cedar tree and looked her straight in the eye. "And when that bunch of girls stole those disks—*your* disks—they also stole my bag." He folded his arms in front of him. "Look, is this some kind of private school prank?"

"I don't know what you're talking about."

"You know, you and your rich friends lure some poor, working-class guy up to your exclusive little neighborhood and mess him up." Amanda opened her mouth to protest, but he cut her off. "Well, if it is, the joke's over. Pay me what you owe me, and I'll be on my way."

"I can't," Amanda shouted in frustration. "I gave you all I had for the delivery." She pointed her finger accusingly in his face. "Which *you* didn't make!"

"Because I was mugged!"

The two of them didn't even notice Pepper walk up beside them. She waved her hand between them and said, "Break it up, you guys."

They pulled away and faced each other with crossed arms. Pepper looked from one to the other and shook her head. "Amazing. You've only known each other for less than an hour and already you're fighting. Must be true love."

For the second time that day, Amanda wanted to throttle her friend. "It's true *something*, all right," Amanda muttered between clenched teeth. "But it's *not* love."

"Ditto," Mick grumbled fiercely.

"Well, as soon as you two end your little quarrel," Pepper said, "I've got a few more important things to talk about."

Amanda glared at Mickey Soul, absolutely infuriated by him. *Whatever possessed you to think he was attractive?* she asked herself. Finally she broke away from their staring contest. "What could be more important?"

"Well, let's start with the flat tire on your scooter," Pepper said. "The air didn't just suddenly leave it. Your tire was slashed."

"Slashed?" Amanda repeated.

Pepper nodded. "And whoever did the slice job on your tires also carved warnings on your locker."

"Hey, what's going on here?" Mick asked.

"Something incredibly rotten," Josh answered, joining them. "My whole backup system has been sabotaged."

Pepper gasped in horror. "You mean, while we were out here in the parking lot, someone was in the Journalism building?"

Josh nodded grimly. "The whole issue is gone. They

nuked it right out of memory. We have to start all over."

Pepper shook her head. "I'm not starting *anything* over until we find out what is going on." She paced back and forth on the gravel drive. "First Mandy gets these threatening notes, then we discover the letter opener stabbed through the paper, then Mick gets attacked—"

"Wait a minute, let's back up," Mick interrupted. "You lost me right around the part where Mandy started receiving threatening notes." He shook his head in disbelief. "Are you talking *life*-threatening notes?"

"'Kill the story, or I'll kill you' sounds pretty life-threatening to me," Pepper said.

"Oh, Pepper, stop being so dramatic," Amanda muttered. "For all we know, it's just a joke."

"Mandy, I'm serious!" Pepper declared. "Whoever's behind this means business."

"Do you know what 'kill the story' means?" Mick asked.

Amanda nodded her head. "In newspaper talk, when you kill a story, you don't publish it. You drop it. You don't pursue it any further."

"So what is it they want you to drop?"

"A series of articles I wrote about the sororities at Sutter Academy—we think," she explained.

Mick raised his eyebrows skeptically. "That's it?"

Amanda nodded. "As far as we can figure out. That's the last article I wrote."

There was a long silence. Finally Josh spoke up. "I think you should kill it, Mandy."

"No!" Amanda shook her head adamantly.

"Amanda, are you going to risk your life just for the paper?" Pepper demanded. "That's idiotic."

"I'm not being stupid about this," Amanda replied. "I think we have to keep running the series, if only to find out who's doing this."

"But why take any chances?" Josh protested.

"Why?" Pepper threw up her hands in the air. "Because she's Amanda Hart, Super Reporter! And because she's stubborn and bullheaded."

"Well, I think we should call the police," Josh said. Pepper nodded vigorously. "I agree."

"And tell them a bunch of girls pushed over a guy on his bike and he skinned his elbow?" Mick said, keeping his eye on Amanda. "And then say those same girls had the nerve to write a few mean notes, telling you to stop writing about their sororities." He laughed sarcastically. "Yeah, the cops will go for that in a *big* way. They'll probably send ten squad cars right over."

His sarcasm rubbed Pepper the wrong way. "Okay, wise guy." She shoved her glasses up on her nose. "You got any better ideas?"

Mick shrugged. "Maybe. I need to think about it."

"While you're *thinking*, I'm going to call the police," Pepper retorted.

"Wait a minute, Pepper, please!" Amanda slumped down under the cedar tree and hugged her knees to her chest. "Mick's right on one thing," she said. "We've got to think this through."

"Right," Mick agreed, sliding down beside her. "I'll help you any way I can."

For the second time that day she noticed how long his lashes were. His clear blue eyes seemed to radiate warmth and concern. The sound of his voice was reassuring and strong.

What am I doing? Amanda asked herself in irritation. *Within five minutes of meeting this guy we're at each other's throats, and now I'm looking at his eyelashes again. Get it together, Hart!*

"I don't know how to put this any other way," she said, forcing herself to be cool. "But this really isn't your problem." Amanda sat upright and added in a businesslike fashion, "Thanks for the offer, but no thanks. We'll take care of this ourselves."

"Whoa, hang on!" Mick broke in. "I'd say this is very much my problem. As of this moment, I am the only person who's suffered any bodily injury. Not to mention the number they did on my bike." He stood up and faced the three of them. "I'm going to find out who did this to me, and make 'em pay for it. So we can work together on this thing, or apart. Either way, I'm going to get to the bottom of it."

"Personally, I think we need all the help we can get," Josh said.

"I don't know." Amanda felt confused. Her emotions were battling inside her. One part of her wanted to trust Mick, but another sent up huge warning signals.

"Oh, come on, Mandy," Pepper urged. "What have we got to lose?"

Josh nodded. "Let's come up with a plan of action."

Amanda spoke slowly. "First we'll have to tell Mr. Mooney some excuse about why this issue of the *Sutter Spectator* won't come out."

"That's easy," Josh said. "I'll say there was a spike in the power supply and the software was damaged." He made a face and added, "Which is basically what happened. It'll take me a few days to reprogram."

"But what'll we do in the meantime?" Pepper asked.

"Maybe I should write up a short announcement to inform everyone about the canceled—I mean, postponed—issue." Amanda's eyes glinted in the fading light. "The announcement will be our bait. I'll make it sound like the next issue of the *Spectator* will have something in it so *hot*, that the kids will be dying to buy it." Amanda looked around the little circle. "If that doesn't flush him—or her—out, I don't know what will."

"It's going to be a little hard for any of you to snoop around," Mick observed. "You start poking around, asking questions, and that'll alert your prey for sure."

"That's a chance we have to take," Amanda said.

"Not necessarily," Mick replied. "I've got an idea."

They all looked at him expectantly.

He glanced down at his watch and frowned. "Hey, I've got to go. I'll have to catch you later." Mick leaped to his feet and picked up his battered bicycle.

"Just a minute," Pepper shouted. "You haven't told us your plan."

"I bet he doesn't *have* one," Amanda muttered under her breath.

"You'll find out." Mick flipped his bicycle up on its rear wheel and straddled the handlebars.

"You're not planning on riding that thing, are you?" Amanda asked. "I thought you said it was trashed."

Mick didn't reply. With a sudden jerk he rose onto the bike as if it were a unicycle. Balancing on the handlebars, he wheeled off down the driveway. Amanda, Pepper, and Josh gasped in amazement.

"Wow!" Josh shook his head as if he couldn't believe what he'd just seen. "That was awesome."

"If he ever gets tired of being a messenger," Pepper remarked, "he can always work in the circus."

"As a clown," Amanda cracked. "I think we've seen the last of that guy."

"You think so?" Pepper sounded disappointed. "I thought he really wanted to help."

"Come on, Pep, he's just a guy off the street," Amanda replied, suddenly feeling tired. "What could he possibly know about Sutter and our lives? We come from totally different worlds, different backgrounds, education—everything." She shook her head. "Who's kidding who?"

"I don't know," Josh said, staring thoughtfully into the distance. "I've got a hunch we may be in for a few surprises."

CHAPTER FIVE

T uesday morning Amanda arrived at Sutter a little late and a little bleary-eyed. She had overslept and barely had time to shower, throw on jeans and a turtleneck sweater, and head out the door. There'd been no time to waste on her hair or makeup. She'd decided to go without her usual light mascara and blush, and had simply pulled her thick brown hair into a ponytail. "Fresh-scrubbed" was the way her Aunt Jane had described her when she came downstairs to grab some orange juice. Amanda hoped she didn't look as awful as that sounded.

The night before Amanda had informed Mr. Mooney about the computer breakdown, and he had accepted Josh's explanation without a second thought. What she hadn't told their advisor was that the three staffers had agreed not to do any work alone in the Coop until the mystery had been solved.

Amanda and Josh had spent most of the night trying to reconstruct the lost edition of the *Spectator* on her Uncle Silas's computer. Fortunately, he was out of town at a physics conference in Denver, so they had been given free rein on his equipment. They were in front of the terminal until the early hours of the morning. Pepper had spent her time locked away in her darkroom at home, reprinting the photos to be used in the issue.

Amanda put one hand to her mouth to stifle a yawn and tried to focus on the combination to her locker. Behind her, several girls had gathered a short distance away. She listened to their conversation with half an ear.

"He is the *hottest* thing to hit Sutter since Matt Carver graduated."

"Matt Carver was *nothing* compared to him. Have you ever seen such eyes?"

"I could just strangle that Whitney Powell!" one girl snapped.

"Yeah—did you see her attaching herself to him like super-glue? I mean, this new guy walks in the door and it's so long, Chip, and hello, Michael."

"Is that his name?"

"What year is he?"

"He's a senior. Can you imagine having to transfer in your last year of school? I'd just hate it!"

Amanda couldn't stand it any longer. She stopped

pretending that she wasn't listening and joined the circle of girls. Several of them were from her junior Composition class.

"I couldn't help overhearing you guys." Amanda smiled her warmest smile. "Is there really a new guy at Sutter?"

"Honey, Michael is not just a *guy*," Cindi Lopez purred. "He is the hottest thing to hit here since—"

Amanda nodded her head. "Since Matt Carver." That was where she had joined the conversation. It sounded like it was going to repeat itself.

"What's his last name?" Maybe Amanda could work this bit of gossip into the notice she was having distributed. As long as the paper was to be delayed, she might as well include some news in the announcement. And a new hunk at school was *always* news.

The girls in the circle all shrugged. "You're not planning on going after him, too?" a pudgy girl named Lynn asked.

Amanda shook her head, and her ponytail swung back and forth. "I haven't even met him."

"Aw, come on." A tall girl with close-cropped blond hair named Ashley sighed. "Give some of us a chance." Ashley turned to her friends. "Hey, I bet Michael doesn't have a date to the Fall Fest."

"Are you kidding?" a familiar voice retorted from the other side of the group. It was Pepper. "Look, if Whitney's already sunk her claws into him, he's probably got not only a date, but dinner reservations for two at the Top of the Mark."

"Pepper, he only got here this morning," Lynn protested.

"Yeah? Let's see . . ." Pepper checked her watch. "The doors opened about an hour ago. He had to talk to the headmistress. That'd take twenty minutes or so . . ."

"So Whitney's had him for half an hour," another girl concluded.

"Half an hour!" Pepper said, putting her hand to her face in amazement. "They're probably engaged."

The bell for first period chimed, and the group dispersed in a gale of laughter. Pepper stepped through them to join Amanda. "I came into the conversation late. What poor guy are we talking about?"

Amanda tossed a few books in her locker and closed it. "Some guy named Michael, with fabulous eyes, who is even hotter than Matt Carver, whoever he was."

Pepper spun to face Amanda. "Hotter than Matt?" Her eyes lit up. "I've got to see this guy." She grabbed Amanda's elbow and dragged her toward the patio. "If Whitney's with him, she's probably parading him around the Hub so all the other guys can see. *Especially* Chip Langsdale."

When they reached the Hub, a crowd of girls were clustered around the fountain.

"I would guess that somewhere inside that mob of females is Michael What's-his-face." Amanda shook her head. "Poor guy. He didn't even make it to his first class before they mobbed him."

A high-pitched giggle soared out of the center of the

milling crowd. "Of course, you *have* to join Key Club," the familiar voice of Whitney Powell could be heard. "Keys and Deltas throw all of the best parties together."

"Well, Amanda, are you just going to stand there?" Pepper asked, nudging her friend with her elbow. "Or should we join the adoring throng?"

"I think I'll sit this one out, thank you." Amanda didn't feel up to meeting the new guy right then. Part of her was curious to see what he looked like, but the other part of her remembered what she looked like— no makeup, a ponytail, jeans and a sweater. Not exactly stylish.

"Hey, Hart." A tanned hand lightly punched her on the shoulder. "If you can't hear my voice, can you read my lips?"

Amanda realized she'd been daydreaming and blinked herself back into focus. A lean, muscular girl with sun-bleached curly hair was grinning at her. "Bonnie!" Amanda murmured. "I'm sorry. I was thinking."

"Don't do that, you could strain something." Bonnie Branch threw her head back and laughed heartily at her joke. Even in her olive green knit dress she looked like an athlete. She was the only girl at Sutter who managed to stay tanned all year round without going to a tanning salon. In San Francisco, with its changeable weather, that was no mean feat. Amanda attributed it to the long hours Bonnie spent on the tennis courts.

Amanda smiled and pointed to the group of girls by the fountain. "So, have you met the new heartthrob?"

"Naw." Bonnie shook her head. "I'm not interested. Besides, from the sound of things, Whitney has him claimed."

"But what about Chip?"

"They're on the outs—again. I guess he committed the unpardonable sin of looking at another girl after the football game last night."

A thought occurred to Amanda. Monday was the day the mugging had taken place. Sutter had played a special make-up game with a school in San Mateo. As a rule, students wanting to attend those away games were allowed out of their seventh-period classes to ride the booster bus. "Did Whitney go to the game yesterday?"

Bonnie nodded. "She was there along with the rest of the Delts, but I don't think she got there till after the first half."

"Any idea why she was late?" Amanda asked, hoping she didn't sound too nosy.

"No, and I really don't care." Bonnie held up two fingers far apart. "Whitney and I are like this. What is this, part of your sorority article?"

"No, just curious," Amanda replied. "But as long as we're on the subject, what did you think of the first article?"

"The Gams thought it was fine, as far as it went." Bonnie Branch was president of the Gammas, the third sorority at Sutter. Most of the Gammas were like Bonnie, interested in sports. "But you didn't mention any of our athletic accomplishments. I mean, for three years running, we have beaten Entre Nous and Delta Psi in every event on Field Day."

"Really? I didn't know that." Amanda tried to keep an attentive look on her face. Meanwhile she analyzed the new information that Bonnie had provided. Whitney had missed the bus on Monday and arrived late to the game. That would have given her enough time to gather her forces and jump Mick in the parking lot.

"So I hope your next article gives that a little more space," Bonnie finished. Amanda realized she had missed the rest of what Bonnie had said to her.

"I'll certainly try." Amanda figured that remark would cover most requests. Bonnie seemed satisfied with her answer and smiled. "Catch you later."

As Bonnie turned and jogged off toward the west wing, Amanda marveled once again at her muscular calves. *That's a lot of tennis,* she thought. *And maybe some weight training thrown in.* Amanda idly wondered if an athlete like Bonnie would be strong enough to overpower a slim six-footer on a ten-speed. *Yes,* she thought, *especially if she had some help.*

Amanda glanced up with a start as Pepper sat down on the bench beside her with a thud. "Well?" Amanda asked.

"You're not going to believe it." Pepper shook her head and stared straight ahead.

"Better than old Matt Carver, huh?"

"Most definitely." Pepper turned and grinned at

Amanda. "I think you'll like him. You two have a lot in common."

Amanda folded her arms. "How do you know? Did you talk to him?"

"I didn't have to."

"Then how can you say—?"

Pepper interrupted her and pointed across the Hub to where the crowd was breaking up. "Look."

There, leaning with one foot against the side of the fountain, wearing a pair of tan chinos, a pale pink striped shirt, and blue blazer, was an incredibly handsome boy. His blue eyes met Amanda's, and the barest smile of recognition crossed his lips.

"I *don't* believe it," Amanda murmured.

"I didn't, either," Pepper whispered out of the side of her mouth. "But it's him."

Gone were the torn jeans and faded T-shirt from Monday. The unruly lock of dark hair that hung sexily over one eye was brushed neatly back off of his forehead. He slipped a pair of dark mirrored sunglasses onto his nose and gave them a jaunty wave.

"Mick—?" Amanda started to say, but Pepper pinched her leg hard and the words came out, "Mick—*OUCH!!*"

"The name's Michael," he said, smoothly stepping across the patio to join them. "Michael Soultaire."

Amanda was speechless with amazement. Even his walk was different. Gone was the easy rolling gait of a guy more comfortable in Reeboks and jeans. Now he moved with the erect poise and grace of an aristocrat.

"What's he doing here?" Amanda hissed in Pepper's ear.

Several girls still remained on the patio, just out of earshot. Pepper only smiled and murmured between her teeth. "He's going to school. What does it look like?"

Amanda made a face at her friend. She turned to Mick and whispered, "Is this your idea of a joke?"

Mick shook his head. He bent over to brush some dust off his pant leg and said quietly, "You needed a bodyguard. I found one."

"A bodyguard?" Amanda blurted.

"Keep your voice down," Mick said. "You'll blow my cover."

"Cover?" Amanda exclaimed.

"Shhh!" Pepper and Mick hushed her.

Amanda lowered her voice and said, "But someone may recognize you!"

"Looking like this?" Mick replied.

Pepper coughed loudly into her hand. "Mandy, he's right," she said. "Look at him. It's like night and day."

"So what do you intend to do with this charade?" Amanda challenged, folding her arms in front of her.

"I thought I'd start off by attending my European History class." Mick pushed back his sleeve and checked his watch. "My, my," he clucked. "I'd better hurry. Hate to be late to my first class."

"Class!" Amanda leaped to her feet. "But . . . How can . . . I mean, this is a private school!" she sputtered. "With rules . . . teachers . . . you need to know how to behave—"

"Michael certainly doesn't need a newcomer like *you* to show him around," Whitney interrupted, slipping her arm into Mick's.

"Where'd she come from?" Amanda muttered to Pepper out of the side of her mouth. Pepper picked up a flat rock lying by the door, looked under it, then shrugged.

Whitney looked as if she had just stepped out of *Seventeen* magazine. She shook her head, fluffing her rich auburn hair over her shoulders. As usual, it was perfectly set and gleamed as though she'd just come from a salon. She had on a short jean skirt with a matching jacket. The white lace camisole underneath gave the whole thing an alluring look. Standing beside her, Amanda felt like a frump.

"Don't mind Amanda, Michael," Whitney said, leaning against his arm. "Just because she writes a column for the newspaper, she thinks she can run people's lives." Whitney turned and stared at Amanda, a hard light in her eyes. "Better be careful, though. She may do an exposé on you, revealing your deepest, darkest secrets."

"Oh, yes, be careful about revealing secrets," Amanda said, trying to catch Mick's eye and warn him. "You never know who might turn them against you."

But he was too busy enjoying Whitney's attention. Mick walked off with Whitney without a backward glance. As they rounded the corner she heard his husky voice say, "I'll keep that in mind, Amanda." The chime of the second bell put a period on his sentence.

"Ooh, he makes me mad!" Amanda stomped her foot in frustration.

"Why?" Pepper asked. "Because he's gazing *soul-fully* into Whitney's baby blues, and not into your emerald greens?"

Amanda rolled her eyes. "Are you kidding? What-ever Mick—*excuse me*—Michael Soultaire does with his time is his own business." She shrugged her shoulders indifferently. "And if he wants to fall for a phony ditz with dyed red hair, that's his option."

"So you *are* upset about it."

"I'm upset because . . . because . . ." Amanda looked around her at the deserted patio and suddenly gasped. "Because first period has begun and we are late!" She ran across the tiles toward Main Hall.

"Amanda, wait!" Pepper called, scrambling to catch up to her. The two girls ran into the east wing and clattered down the hall.

"I can't believe it!" Amanda muttered. "Today we're having a test, and Mr. Phillips hates it when people are late."

"We haven't decided what we should do next," Pepper reminded her.

"I've decided," Amanda said, pausing with her hand on the doorknob to her class.

"What?"

"First I'm going to flunk this stupid algebra test." Amanda clenched her teeth and declared, "And then I am going to personally *strangle* Mr. Michael Soultaire!"

CHAPTER SIX

B efore heading to the cafeteria for lunch, Amanda posted her last notice on the bulletin board in Main Hall. It announced the ticket sales for the Fall Fest dance, the delay of the paper, and had a special message from the editor. Amanda read it out loud. "Sutter Sororities—What Are They Hiding? Read all about it in the next issue of the *Spectator*, where Amanda gets to the Hart of the matter."

Then Amanda pushed open the door of the cafeteria and was hit by a deafening wall of noise. The lunchroom at Sutter was located in what used to be the ballroom of the original mansion. Now the big open room was packed with chattering students, jostling for places at the rows of long tables. She took a place in

line and idly scanned the crowd as she followed the
kids in front of her toward the cash register.

Sutter was like every high school in the world in
that groups of kids staked out certain tables at the beginning of each year, then sat at them every day. Each
of the sororities had claimed tables in a separate corner of the room. The table by the window was re-
served for the jocks, with the cheerleaders encamped
nearby. Student government types took over the tables by the door. The Drama Club naturally sat in the
center of all the action. The rest of the tables were for
the undecided.

Amanda preferred to table-hop because it gave her a
chance to keep up with the latest news around Sutter.
Her column was often filled with little tidbits of information she'd overheard in the lunchroom—funny
comments, new jokes, or some worthy cause that
needed mentioning. At some point during the lunch
hour, Pepper and Amanda hooked up at the table in
the far corner to compare notes.

Pepper was already there, eagerly awaiting her arrival. Amanda paid for her yogurt and fruit and made a
beeline for their table.

"It's about time," Pepper said. "I have been waiting
to talk to you all morning. I saw the announcement."

"What did you think?" Amanda slid her tray onto
the table and sat down across from Pepper.

"I think you are out of your mind—cuckoo—for
printing that about the sororities." Pepper took her
spoon and scooped a bite of Amanda's fruit and yogurt.

"And it won't be too long before you hear from them again."

Amanda took a sip of her diet soda and smiled. "That's the idea. I don't like cowering and waiting. I want to get this thing out in the open, and over with—"

Amanda stopped as she realized Pepper wasn't listening. The redhead was watching something behind Amanda. Without moving her lips, Pepper said, "Warning. Warning. The Greaseman at six o'clock."

Amanda turned to see Jason Stuart rolling up to their table. He was carrying a lunch tray piled high with two jumbo burgers and several orders of french fries.

"There you are," Jason huffed. He set his tray on the table next to Amanda with a clatter.

"It's a direct hit," Pepper cried, cupping her hands around her mouth. "Pow!"

Jason watched her slump forward onto the table and shook his head. "Pepper Larson, you are weird."

Pepper sat up and snatched one of his fries. "Stuart, if I'm weird, you are mondo beyond-o."

"Hey!" Jason yanked his tray out of her reach and turned back to Amanda. "I saw the delay notice about the *Spectator*. I assume that's so you can make room for my Science Fair article."

"Actually, the disk with the issue accidentally got trashed," Amanda said, watching him carefully. "So we have to start from the beginning."

"Great!" Jason nodded his head, definitely pleased. "I'll be able to make the deadline after all." Jason picked up his tray. "This has made my day."

Pepper shook her head in disgust. "I don't believe you. We lose the paper, and you could care less."

"No one seemed to care about my scholarship chances," Jason retorted. "Why should I care about your little problem?"

Amanda and Pepper watched him waddle off smugly and join the table claimed by the science freaks. They were all terribly smart and had strange and wonderful senses of humor. Amanda usually enjoyed their company. Today they just looked like clones of Jason Stuart.

"You know," she said, "sometimes I don't like him very much."

"Sometimes!" Pepper shoved her glasses up on her nose. "Try every minute of the day. I also don't trust him." She leaned forward and whispered, "I think we should move him to the top of the list of suspects for sabotaging the paper and sending you those notes."

"He certainly had a motive." Amanda dipped into her carton of yogurt thoughtfully. "But what about the gang of girls who jumped Mick—excuse me, Michael Soultaire." She rolled her eyes when she said the new name.

Pepper shrugged. "Maybe Jason has sisters. Of course, that's hard to believe. I am convinced he was hatched from some prehistoric egg."

"You know, you're right."

"That he was hatched from an egg?"

"No!" Amanda laughed. "But we've been thinking the girls were from Sutter. They could have been from anywhere. Hired thugs. We don't even know how old they were."

"We should ask Mick." Pepper looked around the lunchroom. "Where is he, anyway?"

"I don't know, and I don't care. I spent the entire morning worrying about him and, as a result, almost flunked a test, completely zoned out a lecture in O'Brien's World Religions, and now have a full-fledged stomachache." Amanda pushed her tray away from her. "You want this?"

Pepper was already dipping into the strawberries with her spoon. "Thanks. Don't mind if I do."

Amanda leaned her chin on her hand. "There's one thing I can't figure out."

"Just one?" Pepper mumbled with her mouth full.

"How did Mick manage to register at Sutter?" She shook her head. "It seemed to be an endless process when I enrolled last year. Forms to fill out about my parents, my grades—all of that. I just don't see how he cut through all of that red tape."

Pepper swallowed. "All I can say is that he is some kind of magician. Either that, or he bought his way in."

"With what?" Amanda asked. "All the money he earns delivering messages on that beat-up old bike?"

"Good afternoon, Miss Wilson!" some kids at the table next to them suddenly called out. Soon the cry echoed around the room. Amanda and Pepper looked up to see May Wilson, the headmistress at Sutter Academy, moving among the tables, greeting and chatting with the students. It was a daily ritual and her way of staying in touch with the student body.

The headmistress was almost revered by the students, but few ever got past her formidable reserve. Amanda was one of the exceptions. From her first day at Sutter, Amanda had felt a special rapport with the older woman.

The petite silver-haired woman stopped at their table and Amanda smiled up at her. "Good afternoon, Miss Wilson."

"Amanda!" Miss Wilson returned the greeting with equal warmth. "I wanted to tell you how impressed I was by Michael Soultaire during our interview this morning."

Pepper nearly choked on the remains of the strawberries and Amanda coughed. "Really?"

"Oh, yes." Miss Wilson folded her hands in front of her. "So well mannered and poised!" She chuckled and added, "In one morning he has managed to charm half the school."

Amanda quickly regained her composure and nodded pleasantly. "Yes, I noticed that, too. I was thinking of doing a feature on him for the paper."

Miss Wilson clapped her hands together. "What a marvelous idea! I'm sure he has some fascinating stories to tell about his travels in Europe."

"I'm sure he does," Amanda said, keeping her smile frozen in place. Meanwhile Pepper kept mouthing silently, "Travels in Europe?" until Amanda kicked her under the table.

"Well, I'd better finish making my rounds." Miss Wilson patted Amanda on the shoulder. "I just wanted to let you know how pleased we are to have Michael here at Sutter. I'm sure your cousin will make a wonderful addition to this school."

"*Cousin!?*" Amanda exclaimed as soon as the headmistress was out of earshot. "Did you hear what she said? Cousin!"

Pepper was clutching her stomach and laughing too hard to answer. Amanda grabbed the empty yogurt carton and threw it at her friend. "This is not funny. That guy could get me in trouble." She slammed her fist on the table. "Ooh, I'd like to strangle him. I'd like to wrap my hands around his throat—"

"And what?" Mick's husky voice whispered in her ear.

It surprised Amanda so much that she knocked her tray off the table, and her soda spilled all over the floor. "Now look what you made me do!" Amanda grabbed a napkin from the metal container on the table and knelt down to wipe up the spill.

"Whoa!" Mick knelt beside her and put his hand on hers. "Chill."

Amanda yanked her hand away and dabbed furiously at the floor. "Ever since I met you, my world has been crumbling around me. You are supposed to be investigating anonymous threats, not creating a public nuisance."

"I *am*," Mick protested. "Investigating, that is." He looped his arm through hers and helped her to her feet. "I'm scoping out the whole sorority scene."

Amanda pushed a strand of hair out of her eyes roughly. "Yeah, I'll bet you are, *cousin!*"

Mick's eyes widened. "You heard?"

"News spreads fast around here." Amanda folded her arms across her chest. "What's the idea of saying you're my cousin?"

Mick shrugged. "I needed a ticket into the academy. Being your relative seemed to do the trick." Mick held his arms out to the sides. "Hey, it's cool. I only told Miss Wilson. No one else knows."

Just then Whitney looped her arm through his. "What's the idea of holding out on us, Amanda? You never told anybody that Michael was your cousin. We had to find out from Miss Wilson."

"Well, actually, he's my second cousin." Amanda smiled sourly at Mick. "Twice removed."

"Michael, I wanted to be the first to invite you to the Delta Tuesday mixer," Whitney said. "It's at my house."

"I'll check my engagement calendar," Mick replied, casually loosening the knot of his tie. "And let you know."

"You do that." Whitney's hand lingered a moment on Mick's arm, and then she turned and strolled back to her table by the window.

Mick raised a hand and called across the lunchroom. "Yo, Whitney!"

The sorority president turned and smiled. "Yes?"

"All right if my cousin comes along?"

Whitney looked disdainfully at Amanda and shrugged. "I suppose. If she has to."

Amanda could feel her face turning red to the very roots of her hair. Alternating waves of humiliation and anger poured over her. Drawing upon all of her self control, Amanda called to Whitney, "I doubt I'll have the time, but thank you for the invitation."

Without waiting for Whitney's response, Amanda picked up her tray and left the table. As she passed Mick she murmured, "I'd like to see you in the hall. Now."

Amanda dropped off her tray and stepped out into the hall. Pepper and Mick followed without a word. Once they were in the deserted corridor, Amanda turned on Mick.

"How *dare* you?" she hissed, her eyes ablaze with fury. "Making me look like some little geek tagalong!"

"Hey, I thought it would be a good chance to do some more investigating." He flashed a smile. "And get in a little partying on the side."

"I don't feel like partying," Amanda snapped.

"Look at it this way. Whitney and her Delta friends are at the top of your suspect list, right?"

Amanda nodded.

"It would be stupid not to check them out, and a party's the best way to do it."

"He's got a good point, Amanda," Pepper admitted.

"I could go alone," Mick pointed out. "But I figured that if the two of us were there, we'd cover that much more ground."

"I'll get my own invitations and dates, thank you very much," Amanda said between clenched teeth.

"Suit yourself. I thought you were serious about getting to the bottom of this."

"Serious? Oh!" Amanda turned her back on him and said to Pepper, "Never in a hundred billion years would I go to a party with him! Not if he were the last person on this earth."

Mick shoved his hands in his pockets and leaned over her shoulder. "So, should I take that as a no?"

Amanda growled, "You can take it as a *never!*"

"Right." He glanced at his watch and said, "Hey, got a hot Math class after lunch. Better get moving." He turned and headed off down the corridor. Just before he disappeared around the corner, Mick called out, "I'll meet you at the flag pole after school."

Amanda squealed with frustration.

"Take it easy, Amanda!" Pepper exclaimed.

"Take it easy? What's he trying to do? Ruin my life completely?"

The two girls walked toward Amanda's locker. "Boy, he really gets to you," Pepper said.

"I have never met a more arrogant, cocky, conceited egomaniac in all my life."

"And those are his good points."

Amanda glared at her friend. "You're a lot of help."

"I just don't see what you're getting so excited about."

"He said he came here to work on the case," Amanda replied. "Well, I think he has his own plan."

"What do you mean?"

"I think Mr. Michael Soultaire is just using us to

meet girls." She paused in front of her locker for a moment. "Do you remember yesterday he said, 'The only people I ever see are old ladies and men in business suits'?" Amanda spun the combination lock furiously. "Boy, were we fooled!"

Pepper leaned against the neighboring locker. "If I didn't know you better, I'd say you were jealous."

"Jealous! Of what?"

"Of Whitney Powell. And every other girl in Sutter who's been hanging all over Mick since he showed up."

"You're the one who was so hot for him," Amanda challenged.

"I know when I'm defeated," Pepper said. "Mick's got his eye on you, and I think you like it."

Her friend's words hit Amanda like a splash of cold water. Could Pepper be right? Amanda took three deep breaths and tried to answer logically.

"Maybe you're right, I don't know. I mean, I'll admit he is attractive. But not my type at all. He's so . . . rough, unsophisticated. And we don't know anything about him. I mean, is he really trying to help us, or is he just a con man?" Amanda opened the door of her locker. "He's certainly not afraid to take chances. The way he just waltzed into this school like he owned—"

Amanda turned her head. Pepper wasn't even paying attention. She just stood there with her mouth open, pointing at the open locker.

There, hanging from the coat hook, was a doll. A noose was wrapped around its neck. Pinned to the pink pinafore was a note on pale blue stationery that read:

YOU ARE ASKING FOR IT!

CHAPTER SEVEN

We have to have a meeting," Pepper said, grabbing Amanda after school that afternoon. She ushered her out of the front gates of Sutter and whispered, "I told Josh and Mick to meet us at Groucho's."

"This afternoon?" Amanda asked. "I thought Mick was going to the Delta mixer at Whitney's."

Pepper shrugged. "He seemed to think this was more important."

Amanda couldn't help feeling pleased at the news.

The popular hangout was only a few minutes' walk from Sutter toward Union Street. As they stepped through the doors of the bustling burger joint, Amanda noticed how tattered the oldtime movie posters decorating the walls were looking. They hung from every available inch of wall space, and life-size cutouts of silent movie greats hung from the rafters. Canvas-backed director's chairs circled wooden tables placed in the center of the room and along the glass window front.

Deep booths lined the back walls, and Amanda looked to see if any were free. They were the best place to talk in private and still keep an eye on the rest of the room.

"There they are," Pepper murmured. Amanda saw the two boys sitting in the booth nearest the kitchen.

Amanda slid into the shiny red booth next to Josh, and Pepper sat next to Mick. Menus printed on black chalkboards, like the kind used to mark the start of a movie scene, lay at each place. They ordered some colas and fries from the waitress, then Pepper said, "I thought this would be a good place to watch our suspects." She gestured to the crowd of students clustered around the tables and video games. A number of the boys had Sutter letter jackets. "This is one of the 'in' places to meet after school."

"That's right." Amanda nodded. "If you miss anybody in the halls, you can always catch them here."

Pepper leaned forward and whispered, "Groucho's is also the main sorority hangout."

At that moment, Bonnie Branch, dressed in black training shorts and carrying a bicycle helmet under her arm, entered the restaurant. Several girls in identical outfits followed her to a nearby table.

Amanda noticed the look of admiration on Mick's face as he watched the athlete slide into her seat.

"Bonnie Branch," she said roughly. "President of the Gammas. And *definitely* a suspect."

Mick smiled. "Gammas, huh? Perfect name."

"Oh?" Amanda arched an eyebrow.

"She's got great gams." He saw the confused look on Amanda's face and added, "Translated—that's great legs."

"You think so?" Amanda heard herself say. "I thought they were a little on the overmuscled side."

Mick shook his head. "Nothing wrong with muscles. Right, Josh?"

Josh blushed so his ears turned red, but he had a big smile on his face. "Right."

"Be careful. Those muscles may have been responsible for your ruined bike and the damaged computer program." Pepper raised her camera to one eye and focused on the room at large.

Mick pointed to one of the Gammas, who was taking off her helmet. A cascade of shiny blond hair tumbled onto her shoulders. "Those girls?" He shook his head. "Never."

"I wouldn't be so sure if I were you, Michael Soultaire," Amanda said. "Looks can be deceiving."

"Gloria has won the triathlon at Sutter two years in a row," Josh explained, gesturing to the tall blond.

"You're kidding?" Mick exclaimed. "Awesome."

Amanda cleared her throat loudly. "If you boys are quite through drooling, we can get down to the business of cracking this case." She lay the pale blue note on the table. "Here's the latest bit of evidence."

Mick picked up the note and examined it carefully.

The humor that usually sparkled in his blue eyes disappeared. He turned it over and over in his hands. "I don't like the sound of this."

"What should we do?" Pepper asked.

"Let's go over this in order," Amanda said. "So far we've had threats, an attack—"

"Two attacks," Josh interjected. "One on Mick, and one on the PC mainframe. Not to mention the letter opener through last week's issue and your slashed tire."

Amanda smiled at her cousin and ruffled his hair. "Okay, *numerous* attacks."

"We know they want to stop the paper from being published," Pepper added, "and we're pretty sure it's because of the sorority article."

"But we don't have any idea who is doing it and what they're afraid the article is going to uncover." Amanda nibbled on her pen. "Is that all we know?"

"We know they're serious." Mick folded the note neatly and set it on the table. "They've also made it clear that they have every intention of stopping you from publishing that article."

"I think we can be pretty certain that whoever it is goes to Sutter," Josh chimed in.

"How can you be so sure?" Mick asked.

Amanda shrugged. "Who else would be interested in a silly article in a school newspaper?"

"Try a blond guy with stringy hair and a tattoo on his hand," Pepper declared. She still had her camera held up to her eye and was now focusing on a figure standing outside the restaurant. "He's been leaning against that parking sign watching us ever since we came in."

Without looking up, Mick said, "I know." Amanda looked at him in surprise. "He was hanging around outside the entrance to the school this morning. And when Josh and I left Sutter this afternoon, he was waiting in the bushes near the front gate. He must have followed you here."

Amanda felt as though an arctic wind had just blown through the room. "I don't like this," she muttered, "I don't like it at all. What should I do?"

Mick took a deep breath. Finally he said, "Be careful."

"Oh, great, that's a lot of help." Amanda threw her hands in the air. "Well, that solves everything. Just be careful."

Mick took one of her hands. "No. I mean, take precautions." His voice was low and serious. He turned to look at Josh. "That's where you come in. Never let Amanda walk to school by herself."

Josh nodded solemnly. "I won't."

"Once you're in school, I'll walk you to all of your classes," Mick went on.

"Won't that interfere with you and Whitney?" As soon as the words had left her mouth, Amanda wanted to kick herself. She was starting to sound like a jealous girlfriend.

Mick smiled his sexy half-smile and said, "Naw, I'll see her in class." Amanda narrowed her eyes and he held up one hand. "Hey, I was just kidding! You forget why I'm here. I'm your bodyguard."

"I just want to make sure *you* don't forget," Amanda said pointedly.

"Listen, Miss Hart," Mick said, a trace of irritation in his voice, "going to Sutter with a bunch of preppie teeners is not my idea of a great time."

"Nobody's forcing you to stick around," Amanda retorted, crossing her arms.

"*Nobody* is right," Mick snapped. "As soon as my bike is fixed, I'm history."

The click of a camera shutter broke the tension. They turned to see Pepper aiming her lens at them. "You two argue more than my parents," she drawled. "And they're blue-ribbon champs."

No one said anything more as the waitress delivered their drinks and set a basket of fries smothered in cheese and chili peppers in the center of the table.

"Things are really getting weird around this place," Pepper muttered under her breath. "Look at that guy in the black T-shirt. He's got a face that would frighten his own mother."

Amanda looked up and almost did a double take in shock. A stocky guy had come in the door and strode up to the takeout counter. His heavily muscled arms and chest bulged out of his T-shirt, but what made him stand out was his pockmarked face. *Not someone I'd like to meet in a dark alley,* Amanda thought.

Then she received another shock. As the guy stood by the counter, Mick caught his eye and the two of them exchanged the slightest of nods. Josh and Pepper were too busy putting straws into their drinks to notice.

"Who was that?" she asked, delicately unwrapping her straw.

Mick reached across her for the catsup. "Who?"

"That guy who just came in here."

Mick tipped the catsup bottle over the fries and pounded on it. "How should I know?" He glanced up at the stranger and shrugged. "I must have seen him around Sutter, or something."

"That bruiser?" Amanda pointed to the guy, who was now leaning over the jukebox, examining the selections. "Are you kidding?"

Mick stopped pounding on the base of the bottle and shot her a peculiar look. "Why not?"

"Well, look at the way he's dressed," Amanda replied. "They wouldn't let him in the door dressed like that."

"Like what?"

"Come on, Mick," Amanda protested. "He looks like a hood!"

"Really?" His voice dripped with sarcasm. "You must be some kind of genius, to be able to just look at a person and tell whether he's good enough to go to school with you."

"Oh, you know what I mean."

"No, I don't." Mick's voice was the most serious she'd ever heard it. "What you're saying is, the only way into a place like Sutter is to have the right wardrobe. Is that it?"

"That's not it at all," Amanda protested angrily. "This whole conversation has gotten completely off the track." She took a sip of her drink and banged it down on the table in frustration. "All I wanted to know was whether you knew that guy or not."

Mick, who was still struggling with the catsup bottle, gave it a sharp slap, and a red stream shot across the table onto Amanda's sweater. She leaped to her feet, knocking over her cola.

"Hold it, I think it's going to be a good one," Pepper said as she snapped Amanda's picture.

"Come on, Pepper, not now!" Amanda wiped furiously at her sweater.

"Good photographers capture life's real moments," Pepper replied. "And that was certainly real."

Amanda gave up on the catsup and grabbed some napkins to sop up the soda dripping onto the booth and floor. "Sometimes I wish you wouldn't try so hard to be good."

Pepper grinned and the shutter clicked again.

"Geez, Amanda, I'm really sorry," Mick said, kneeling to help her. "Will it come out?"

"It better. I need to try to wash it off."

"I'll go to the ladies' room with you," Pepper said.

Mick, who was still mopping up the spill on the floor, cracked, "Josh, my man, have you ever noticed how girls can never go to the bathroom alone? Why is that?"

"Because we intend to talk about you," Pepper shot back. She set her camera down in front of Josh. "Guard this with your life, and maybe when we get around to discussing you, we'll be kind."

Amanda led the way across the room to the dark pink door marked with a silver star. The interior of the bathroom was decorated to look like a movie star's dressing room. The two girls passed through the small lounge with its chaise and small vanity table into the bathroom itself. Round globes of soft light ringed the mirror above the sink. Amanda leaned against it and turned on the cold water tap. "If I didn't know better, I'd think he squirted me on purpose."

"Now, why would he want to do that?" Pepper asked, tearing off a handful of paper towels and handing them to her friend. Amanda caught a glimpse of herself in the mirror and groaned.

"Pepper, why didn't you tell me I looked this awful?" Her dark hair was still pulled back in a ponytail, but little wisps hung down all around her face.

Pepper stepped behind her and gazed into the mirror. "You look fabulous. A natural beauty."

"Fabulous? My hair's a wreck, my clothes are awful, and I now have an attractive spot of catsup covering the front of my sweater."

"Things could be worse." Pepper draped her arm around her friend's shoulder and spoke to her reflection. "You could be short, nearsighted, and have lost the war of the freckles."

Amanda crossed her eyes goofily. Pepper stuck out her tongue. Amanda and Pepper were so busy laughing and making faces that at first, they didn't hear the voices in the lounge.

"You have got to go through with this," a voice was saying. "You know how important it is to all of us."

Amanda grabbed Pepper by the elbow and pulled her into one of the stalls at the back of the bathroom. She put her finger to her lips and motioned for Pepper to stand on the toilet seat. She eased the door shut and climbed up beside her friend.

One of the girls, whose voice sounded strained from crying, said, "I can't take much more of this."

"You have to," another, stronger voice insisted. "We're all counting on you."

"But I'm scared." The girl started making little hiccupping sounds.

Amanda was dying to peek over the door and see who was arguing. Both voices sounded familiar, but she couldn't quite identify the speakers. It took every bit of Amanda's willpower to stay put.

"Quit crying. It's not going to help," the stronger voice said. "Just do it—or you're *out*." Amanda and Pepper listened to the sound of the paper towel dispenser. "Now, wash your face and dry your eyes. You look terrible."

They listened as the sound of a single pair of footsteps clicked across the tile floor. Then the outer doors swung open and shut, and silence returned to the room.

Ever so slowly Amanda raised her head and peered over the top of the stall. She nearly lost her balance and had to cling to Pepper to keep from falling.

In front of the mirror stood a pale blond girl Amanda recognized as Heather Grey. She was a junior cheerleader and, more important, a member of the sorority Entre Nous. Heather stared at her tear-stained face for a long moment, pulling a brush through her hair with rough strokes. Finally she took a deep breath, jammed the brush back in her purse, and ran out of the bathroom. Amanda and Pepper exploded out of their stall in hot pursuit.

"My car's about a half a block down the street," Pepper whispered as they reentered the restaurant.

Amanda nodded. "I'll grab Mick and Josh and meet you."

When she reached their booth, only Josh was sitting there. "Where's—?"

"Over there," Josh cut her off, a sheepish grin on his face. Amanda glanced in the direction he was pointing and frowned. Mick was standing by the Gammas' table, having an animated conversation with the tall blond named Gloria.

"Come on. We've got work to do," Amanda barked. "Get Mick while I pay the bill."

Moments later Mick was standing beside her at the register. "What's up?" he asked.

"I'm not sure yet." Amanda pointed out the window at Heather, who was hopping into a white Honda Accord. "But she's a key player."

Amanda picked up her change and they ran out onto the sidewalk. She squinted up Union Street into the glaring afternoon light. They heard a loud backfire, and a beat-up yellow Mustang convertible roared into view. It screeched to a halt at the curb and Pepper yelled, "Get in, quick!"

Mick and Josh hopped into the backseat of the old Mustang, and Amanda leaped into the front. Holding on to the top of the windshield, Amanda pointed at the white Honda disappearing around the corner and shouted, "Follow that car!"

CHAPTER EIGHT

H eather found a parking space right on Union Square!" Pepper pounded the steering wheel in frustration. "Not fair!"

"Mick and I'll get out here," Amanda said. She opened the door and stepped out onto the street. "You and Josh park Mustang Sally."

"Oh, terrific," Pepper groaned. "We could be circling for hours."

Amanda pointed to the pale blond crossing Geary Street. "She's heading for I. Magnin. We'd better tail her. That store has ten floors."

"Whoa, wait a minute!" Mick grabbed Amanda by the arm and jerked her back to the side of the car.

"What are you doing?" she said, fuming. "You nearly dislocated my arm."

"You're about to blow our cover." Mick pulled his pair of mirrored sunglasses out of his pocket and slipped them on. "It's important we be cool. Watch me."

Mick, back to his old swagger, strolled between the passing cars across the street. He paused just long enough to buy a paper from a vendor, tucked it under his arm, and then nodded for Amanda to join him. Without another glance at her he disappeared into the department store.

"Honestly." Amanda rolled her eyes at Pepper. "You'd think this was *Miami Vice*."

"Mandy, I think you should trust the guy," Pepper shouted over the noise of the street. "He seems to know what he's doing."

She shoved the yellow Mustang into first gear and peeled out in a cloud of exhaust, leaving Amanda coughing behind her.

Yeah, he does seem to know exactly what he's doing, Amanda thought with a frown. *That's why I wonder who we've gotten ourselves mixed up with!*

Amanda stepped through the glass doors of I. Magnin and surveyed the first floor. There was no sign of Mick anywhere. "He's probably in the lingerie department checking out the mannequins," she muttered to herself. The store was huge and Amanda decided the best place to start looking for Heather was in Cosmetics.

Amanda moved down the aisle, pausing to smooth her hair in a small round mirror that sat on the counter. A few rows away she picked up a tester and dabbed a little Reminiscence behind one ear.

"Caught you," Mick's voice rumbled in her ear. It sent shivers down the right side of her body, and she nearly dropped the test bottle.

"Where've you been?" she whispered.

"Following Heather. She's over in the jewelry department." He turned and sauntered off down the aisle, calling over his shoulder, "Buy that perfume. It smells great on you."

Amanda stifled a smile and returned the tester to its place. She caught up with Mick a few aisles away, and the two of them pretended to examine purses that hung on a large display rack. Amanda looped a small leather bag over her shoulder. "What do you think?"

"I think that our Heather has expensive tastes," Mick replied, pretending to comment on her purse.

Amanda hung the bag back on the display rack and picked up another purse. "She always looks great at school. I think her dad has money."

"Lots of money?"

"Well, yes, I guess so. She's got a car, and all that. I think he's with some bank."

"Then what would a rich girl be doing shoplifting?"

"What?" Amanda gasped.

"Keep it down, will you?" Mick grabbed her arm and forced her to look at one of the purses. She made an elaborate show of examining it with delight. Keeping a broad smile plastered on her lips, she murmured, "How do you know she's shoplifting?"

"Check out the left pocket on her jacket," Mick replied. "It was empty when she walked in. Now it contains a gold necklace."

Amanda turned slowly to catch a sideways glance of Heather trying on various pieces of jewelry. "But . . . but how? The saleslady hasn't left her side."

Mick nodded. "Heather's good."

"You mean, you think she's done it before?"

"No question. She's got the technique down."

Amanda raised one eyebrow. "And what technique is that?"

"It's the shell game—the oldest con in the book."

Amanda shook her head. "I don't get it."

"You've heard how the hand is quicker than the eye? Well, Heather has the saleslady show her several pieces of jewelry. Then she has her put one of them back, selects two more, has the saleslady put one back, asks to see one that was already replaced, and so on. She shuffles them around, all the while talking up a storm. Soon the saleslady doesn't remember how many she's shown Heather. Then Heather diverts her attention by introducing another element."

"Like those scarves?" Amanda gestured with her eyes. Heather was in the process of matching various pieces of jewelry with a selection of silk scarves.

"You're a fast learner. You see, the saleslady is advising her on which necklace to wear with the scarf. So much has now come and gone on the counter that the small gold necklace won't be missed."

"Wow." Amanda moved over to the hat display. Suddenly she tugged on Mick's arm. "Wait a minute. Look, she's buying something."

Mick nodded. "The scarf."

"Well, if she's as good a thief as you say," Amanda

asked, "why would she buy the scarf when she could steal it?"

"Think about it. The scarf costs ten, maybe twenty dollars."

"Or more," Amanda said, looking at a price tag on one of the hats.

"Okay." Mick shrugged. "But I'd say that designer necklace is in the hundreds. Spend a little—get a lot."

Heather moved away from the jewelry counter toward their aisle. Amanda slammed a wide-brimmed hat on her head and faced the mirror. Mick leaned in close beside her and nodded approval. "I like it."

"Well, I don't," Amanda whispered. "Why would a girl like Heather shoplift?"

"Why don't we find out?"

Before she could stop him, Mick was already striding down the aisle. Heather stopped beneath a sign announcing Women's Designer Apparel and began rifling through the racks of expensive outfits. Mick turned and grinned at Amanda. "Nothing but the best for this girl."

Amanda was in a state of shock. Heather Grey was one of the sweetest girls at Sutter, liked by everyone. There was a frail, vulnerable quality about her that was almost old-fashioned. Never in a million years would Amanda have guessed she was a thief.

"My hunch is that she'll probably go for something she can tuck inside the shopping bag she picked up when she bought the scarf," Mick said, observing her from behind a neighboring display. "Something along the lines of a silk blouse, or some lingerie."

Heather passed by the sweaters, giving only a brief glance at the price tags. Amanda held her breath as the girl chatted easily with a saleslady. Then, just as Mick had predicted, Heather headed for the blouses. She found a deep plum one that matched the colors of the scarf she'd bought. Amanda watched as Heather carefully turned to keep the saleslady in view out of the corner of her eye. As soon as the woman turned away to deal with someone else, Heather reached for the blouse.

"I can't stand it," Amanda hissed. "I've *got* to stop her!"

Heather had already removed the hanger and was slipping the blouse into her bag when Amanda put one hand on her arm. "That's not a good idea," Amanda whispered.

Heather's entire body jumped and she dropped the blouse on the carpeted floor. "I don't know what you're talking about." Heather's voice was steady, but her eyes betrayed her fear.

Amanda picked up the blouse and put it back on the hanger. "I know what's in your left-hand pocket." A little twitch in Heather's face confirmed Amanda's fears. With a sinking heart she realized that Mick had been completely right about Heather. "I think you should return it before you leave the store."

"What are you, some kind of store detective?" Heather pretended to keep looking at sweaters, but her hands were shaking.

Amanda watched the girl's trembling hands and said

softly, "I'm just your friend, Heather. You don't need to do this."

"Yes, I do," the pale girl replied in a barely audible voice. "You don't understand."

"Why?" Amanda asked. "If it's the money, I'll lend it to you."

"That's not it at all." Heather's voice had begun to quiver. "They're making me."

"Who, Heather?" Amanda persisted. "Who's making you?"

Suddenly Heather flung her head back, and a cold, hard look came into the girl's eyes. "Nobody's forcing me, okay? It's just an initiation prank for the sorority. Everybody does it."

Heather turned and walked hurriedly down the center of the store toward the street. Amanda followed hot on her heels, throwing questions at her. "Everyone does it? What are you talking about? Look, Heather, you don't have to do anything illegal to be in a sorority. Report them to Miss Wilson. She'll stop it."

"No!" Heather turned on Amanda. "Look, this is none of your business."

"Heather, you're in trouble. You need help."

"You're not my mother!" the other girl hissed. "I can handle this, so *please* just leave me alone!" Heather pulled the necklace out of her left-hand pocket and threw it at Amanda. Then she raced out the front of the department store.

"Heather!" Amanda called after her helplessly. Her shoulders slumped in defeat.

"You tried," Mick said gently, coming up beside her. "At least you stopped her this time."

"I really felt she was going to open up," Amanda said, "but something stopped her."

"Could've been the group from Sutter."

"What?" Amanda turned and stared at him. "I didn't see anybody."

Mick shrugged. "Two girls passed behind you while you were talking to her."

"That explains it!" Amanda exclaimed. "One minute she was this soft, vulnerable girl, and the next minute—"

"A pro." Mick held out the necklace that Heather had thrown. Attached to it was a slim pastel card with the price printed on the inside.

"Three hundred dollars!" Amanda clapped a hand over her mouth.

"Easy, Mandy," Mick chuckled as he looped his arm through hers and guided her back toward the jewelry counter. "If you're not careful, we'll get caught with the goods and take the rap."

"What should we do?" Amanda whispered.

Mick flipped his sunglasses onto his nose. "We cruise by the counter, you create a diversion, and I'll drop it on the glass."

"What kind of diversion?"

Mick cocked a sly smile. "Surprise me."

CHAPTER NINE

E|xcuse me! Please, let me through!" Mick shouted. "I'm her husband." He pushed through the group of customers and clerks that had gathered around Amanda. She lay slumped on the carpet between the jewelry and cosmetics counters.

"Don't you think we should call a doctor?" a short, balding man asked.

"No, it's not necessary," Mick said, bending down to peer at Amanda. "She always faints like this. She has this thing about shopping and crowds."

Mick scooped Amanda up in his arms and smiled at the group. "She'll be just fine once I get her outside."

The people parted to let Mick through, and he moved down the aisle with Amanda in his arms. Her head rested on his shoulder, and one arm was draped across his back.

When they were out of hearing range of the crowd she whispered, "Did I surprise you?"

"Surprise me? You scared the living daylights out of me," Mick hissed.

"Good." Amanda giggled and raised her head to look at him.

"Keep your head down, they're still watching." Mick made his way to the front entrance, nodding to several of the clerks. He murmured, "Did you have to shout, 'Oh, my God, I'm going to be sick'?"

Amanda squinted up at him. "It was either that, or 'Fire!'"

"Well, I guess I was lucky then."

Amanda, still pretending to be unconscious, asked, "Did you put the necklace back?"

Mick nodded. "I dropped it right in the case. Your act was so good, the saleslady left it wide open." He backed through the double doors and stepped out onto Geary Street. "We made it."

Amanda sat up and patted him on the shoulder. "You can put me down now." She hopped lightly out of his arms and added, "Thanks for the lift."

Mick grinned. "My pleasure."

Over Mick's shoulder, Amanda immediately spotted Pepper trying to squeeze the bright yellow Mustang into a tiny parking spot. Josh stood on the sidewalk behind the car, making futile attempts to guide her. Pepper had a fiercely determined look on her face. Several times she pulled the car forward, cranked the steering wheel, and tried to maneuver the car into the little spot.

Amanda chuckled, "Now *there's* a girl who likes a challenge."

"Even a motorcycle would have trouble with that spot," Mick cracked. "Let's stop her before she manages to really park those wheels."

"Yeah," Amanda said, following Mick across the street. "She'll never get out."

"Whoa, Pepper!" Mick called out.

Pepper didn't hear him. Her radio was going full blast, and she was busy cursing and pounding the steering wheel. Mick threw himself on the hood of her car and mouthed the words "We're back!" through the windshield. Pepper shrieked and let go of the wheel, and the car bounced against the curb.

"That was smooth, Pepper." Mick peeked his head over the top of the windshield and grinned. "Ultra-smooth."

Pepper folded her arms across her chest and stared at him. "You have a crazed maniac throw himself against your windshield, and see how calm you are."

"Pepper, he had to stop you, and the usual ways weren't working," Amanda said, climbing into the backseat.

"*Oh*, now you're taking *his* side." Pepper wiggled her eyebrows. "This *is* unusual. What happened in that department store?"

"If you get this crate out of here, we'll tell you." Mick hopped over the windshield and into the front seat as Josh joined Amanda in the back.

"Out's easy." Pepper jammed it into first and after several tries eased out into traffic. Mick, Amanda, and Josh all applauded.

"Okay," Pepper called over her shoulder. "Now that you've all had your first lesson in parallel parking—"

"Is that what that was?" Mick asked with a straight face.

Pepper swiped at him and he ducked.

Amanda called from the backseat, "I just want to remind you that you're the driver and we're the passengers. You're supposed to keep both hands on the wheel."

"Get her." Pepper gestured with her thumb at Amanda. "She's giving lessons and she's never driven a car in her life."

Mick spun in his seat. "You're kidding."

Amanda shook her head. "In Europe, kids can't drive until they're seventeen, maybe eighteen. Everyone uses a scooter or a bike."

Mick folded his arms smugly. "Wise choice."

"I think I'd take the bus," Josh said. "Those people drive like maniacs."

Amanda laughed. "They'd probably say the same thing about us."

"Not us." Mick shook his head firmly. "Just Pepper."

Pepper stuck her tongue out at Mick and then asked, "Well, are you going to tell us what you found out, or do we have to guess?"

"Oh, Pepper, it's bad news." Amanda leaned forward, resting her elbows on the back of Mick's seat. "Heather Grey is a shoplifter."

"You're kidding!" Pepper flicked on the turn signal and headed up the street. "She doesn't seem like the type at all."

"Does anyone in Entre Nous seem like the type?"

Pepper shook her head. "They're so straight, it hurts."

Amanda shrugged. "According to Heather, they're all supposed to shoplift as part of their initiation."

"Wow!" Pepper glanced at Amanda in shock. "Isn't that called hazing, making people do dangerous things to get into a club?"

Amanda nodded.

"I thought most schools outlawed hazing," Josh said. "I read that some students have died because of some of the terrible things they were forced to do."

"I don't think shoplifting could kill you," Mick interjected. "But it could put a serious dent in your social life. Doing time in juvenile hall is the ultimate bummer."

Amanda watched Mick closely as he spoke. Something in the way he said "juvenile hall" made her think he might have had firsthand experience in the place. "Heather said they were making her do it. She was really upset."

"Could have been good acting," Josh said.

"It seemed pretty real to me," Amanda replied.

Mick turned to face Amanda. "Well, we know that this wasn't her first time shoplifting. Her technique was too good."

Once again the disturbing thought ran through

Amanda's mind. *How could he be such an authority on stealing?*

"Maybe she's a kleptomaniac," Josh suggested. "You know, she has to steal and can't stop herself."

"Maybe she is," Pepper admitted. "But what would that have to do with the newspaper, and the threats?"

Amanda sighed. "Maybe she was telling us part of the truth. Maybe it *is* some sort of a hazing thing. And maybe—just maybe—*all* of the sororities are doing it, like she said."

"Talk about a scandal!" Pepper guided the Mustang up the steep grade of Powell Street.

Amanda met Pepper's eye in the rearview mirror and whispered, "And it would be the hottest story ever to run in the *Spectator.*"

The yellow Mustang crested the hill and started to pick up speed as they came down the other side.

"Yo, Pepper, there's a red light coming up," Mick pointed out casually.

"I know." Pepper tapped the brake, then looked up in surprise as the old Mustang didn't respond. "Nothing's happening."

"Come on, Pepper," Amanda urged from the back seat. "Don't kid around."

"I'm not kidding!" Pepper pushed the pedal and it went all the way to the floor. "The brakes are gone."

Amanda and Josh sat frozen in the backseat, watching the stoplight come faster and faster toward them. The intersection was choked with traffic.

"Downshift," Mick ordered. "Now!"

Pepper slammed the gear into second. The car

lurched but kept hurtling down the hill. "It's not working!"

Mick hit the horn, and the cars in the intersection swerved to avoid the runaway car. At the same time he pulled back on the emergency brake. The acrid smell of burning rubber filled the air. The Mustang fishtailed across the street, heading for a group of cars.

"Look out!" Pepper screamed.

Suddenly a large green Pontiac roared up alongside them. Amanda caught sight of the driver and nearly fainted. It was the pockmarked guy she had seen walk into Groucho's.

With a loud crunching sound, the green Pontiac swerved and plowed into the front of the little Mustang.

"What's that idiot trying to do?" Amanda shouted.

The impact made them ricochet to the left. A gap appeared in the traffic, and Pepper aimed the Mustang for it. Miraculously, they shot through the intersection safely, but before they could relax, another crowded traffic exchange loomed ahead of them.

"Oh, my God, a cable car!" Amanda's words died in her throat. The red and black tram seemed to fill the windshield. Then suddenly the menacing green car roared up on their left side and rammed them again.

"He's trying to kill us!" Pepper shrieked.

Mick was still clutching the emergency brake with his left hand. He reached out with his free hand and jerked the steering wheel to the right. Amanda grabbed Josh and covered her face, bracing for the impact with the cable car.

Suddenly it felt as if they were moving in slow motion. The sound of screeching brakes faded away, and Amanda heard only the roar of the wind. The car jostled violently and she opened her eyes. Somehow they had missed the cable car and were bouncing up onto the curb. A large neon sign in the form of a dragon came into view declaring, Chan's Chinese Food To Go. The car bumped past the restaurant and plowed into a huge mountain of green. The impact threw Amanda against the back of the front seat, and then everything was still.

It seemed like hours before any of them moved. Amanda sat very still, listening to her heart pounding in her chest. *I'm alive!* she thought jubilantly.

Amanda realized she was still clutching Josh's hand. Their knuckles were bright white. In the front seat Pepper sat stiff as a board, still gripping the steering wheel with both hands. Mick was the only one who stirred. He waved his hand in front of Pepper's face.

"You okay?" he asked.

Pepper nodded stiffly.

"How about you guys?" He turned to look at Amanda and Josh over the seat. A bright red gash trickled blood down his forehead.

"Mick, your face!" Amanda reached out to touch him.

"It's no big deal." He rubbed his forehead with his sleeve. "I think I caught the edge of the windshield."

Josh slowly turned his head to the left, to the right, and then patted his legs. "No sign of whiplash. All bones are unbroken." He smiled at the group shakily. "I'm okay."

Pepper remained frozen in the same position. Amanda leaned forward and gently shook her friend's shoulder. "Pepper, are you all right?" She shook her shoulder again. "Pepper, speak to me."

Pepper slowly turned her head to look at the group. Only her lips moved. "The next time one of you shouts, 'Follow that car!' I'm taking a bus."

Tears of relief sprang to Amanda's eyes. She wrapped her arms around Pepper and hugged her tightly. "It's a deal."

"Everyone okay in there?"

A small Chinese man in a white apron appeared by the car. Other employees from the restaurant hurried toward them.

"I think so," Mick told the man.

"Boy, this is one big mess," the man in the apron said, shaking his head. Suddenly Amanda realized what the green mountain she had seen was. Dozens of bags of garbage were strewn all over the sidewalk and into the street. They had been stacked for pickup in front of the restaurant and luckily had provided a soft barrier for the careening Mustang. Many of the bags had burst, and their smelly contents lay everywhere.

"I never thought I'd be so happy to see garbage." Amanda laughed. "This big, beautiful mess probably saved our lives."

"Should I call the police?" the man asked, wiping his hands on his apron.

"Please do," Amanda replied.

As the man turned to leave, Mick spun in his seat and hissed. "Why call the cops? All we really need is a tow truck."

"I think we need the police," Amanda insisted. "That green car tried to kill us!"

"Wait a minute!" Mick held up one hand. "That guy saved our lives. If he hadn't rammed us out of the path of that cable car, we would've had Rice-a-Roni printed all over the front of our faces."

Pepper crawled out of the driver's seat and stepped shakily to the front of her car. "Look at the fender," she cried. "It's mushed!"

Mick hopped over the side door and surveyed the damage. He shook his head. "You're going to need some heavy-duty body work. The front end isn't just mushed, it's totaled."

"Totaled?" Pepper slumped against the fender.

"Pepper?" Josh asked, carefully getting out of the car. "When was the last time you checked the brake fluid?"

"Brake fluid?" Pepper bit her lip, trying to remember. "Is that like the oil?"

Mick and Josh exchanged knowing looks. "I'd say she's never checked it," Mick said.

"I may have," Pepper protested. "I'm just not sure when. I do take it in for regular, uh, you know—checkups."

"Tune-ups," Josh corrected.

"Whatever," Pepper retorted. "You know what I mean."

"Look," Mick pointed out, "your windshield wiper is attached with a rubber band, the knob is just duct-taped to the gearshift, and your gas gauge is on empty. I'd say it's pretty likely you didn't check the brake fluid."

While Pepper and Mick argued, Amanda watched Josh kneel down and peer under the car. Finally he lay on his side and slid under the engine.

The reflection of flashing lights in the storefront window announced the arrival of the police. As the officers got out of their patrol car, Pepper scurried to get her purse with her driver's license out of the front seat.

"Josh?" He was still underneath the car. Amanda tugged at her cousin's leg. "The police are here. Better come out of there."

He slid out from under the car and stood up, wiping the remains of lettuce and other bits of garbage clinging to his navy blue pants.

Amanda didn't know why, but she felt scared. She knew they hadn't done anything wrong, but just the presence of policemen made her feel guilty.

She needn't have worried. The officers mostly wanted to make sure none of them had been injured. The taller of the two, a thin, black man with a moustache, asked Pepper to describe the accident in detail. When she got to the part about the mysterious green car, both cops perked up.

"It was a dark green Le Mans," Josh spoke up. "A seventy-eight, I think. It had a dented hood and the paint was not the original color."

"Very observant." The policeman nodded his approval. "How about the driver?"

Josh's face went blank. "I only know cars. I didn't notice the driver. But Mick said the guy was doing us a favor."

"I'd seen him before at Groucho's, on Union Street," Amanda added. Suddenly she remembered the nod Mick had exchanged with the stranger. "I think Mick may have even known him."

"Who's Mick?" the tall policeman asked.

"He's right here." Amanda turned to gesture beside her. "Or he was. Where'd he go?" She spun in a circle, looking up and down the street. There wasn't a sign of him.

The two policemen exchanged looks, and the shorter one asked, "What does this Mick guy have to do with this?"

"Nothing," Josh said quickly. "He was a passenger in our car. Unfortunately, he had a job he had to get to."

"Am I going to get a ticket?" Pepper asked meekly.

"I don't think so," the tall officer said. "No one was hurt. No damage done to anyone else's property."

"What about my garbage?" the Chinese man protested.

"We'll clean it up," Amanda heard herself snap at him. She was starting to get an uneasy feeling in her stomach. She had a lot of questions that needed answering. Finding out that mild little Heather Grey was a thief was bad enough. But why had Mick disappeared the moment the police arrived? What was he afraid of?

The tow truck pulled up just as the police completed their questioning. Pepper rode with the driver to the garage, and Amanda and Josh stayed behind to clean up.

As Pepper clambered into the truck, she muttered, "How am I going to tell my mother about this? How was I supposed to know about brake fluid? I'm just a teenager."

They watched the forlorn hulk that used to be Mustang Sally disappear around the corner. Then Amanda turned and walked up to the Chinese man, who was busy ordering his employees back to work. "Pardon me, Mr. . . . uh . . ."

"Chan," he said, gesturing at the sign.

"Mr. Chan." Amanda smiled. "We said we'd clean up the mess. Do you have any extra bags we could use?"

"Oh, don't worry about it," he said with a wave of his hand. "Go home. You've had enough trouble for today. We'll take care of it."

"Really?" Amanda said gratefully. "That's very kind of you."

They said good-bye and headed for home. "Let's walk for a while. I don't think I could take getting on another moving vehicle just now," Amanda confessed.

The two of them walked in silence, wrapped in their own thoughts. Finally Josh cleared his throat. "Mandy, I don't think you should continue the newspaper articles."

"Where'd that come from?" She blinked at him in surprise.

"Well, I've been putting things together and . . ." He hesitated for a moment, then declared, "I'm worried about your safety."

Amanda put her arm around her cousin's shoulder. "Look. There are a lot of unresolved questions on this thing, but that's no reason to panic."

"No!" Josh declared. "I think we *should* worry. Today confirms it."

"Come on, Josh!" Amanda tried to make light of it all. "So we see a couple of strange guys, we find out Heather and maybe a few other girls are shoplifting, and Pepper forgets to check her brake fluid."

"Pepper *didn't* forget."

"Of course she did. It's just like her. She's always running out of gas and—"

"Mandy, listen to me." Josh stopped and put his hands on her shoulders. "I checked under the car, and what happened to us was no accident."

"Josh, what are you saying?" Amanda couldn't hide the fear in her voice.

"Pepper's brake line was punctured—*deliberately*."

CHAPTER TEN

A manda, you're nuts!" Pepper slammed the piece of paper she had just finished reading down on the pasteup table. "You've just accused *seventy* girls of *stealing* to get into a club."

"I know."

It was Wednesday morning, and Amanda had asked Pepper and Josh to meet her in the Coop before class. She showed them the article she had written the night before.

"You can't print this," Pepper continued. "Parents will yank their kids out of Sutter so fast, their heads will spin."

"Not to mention the fact that it will bring the entire San Francisco police force down on us in a minute,"

Josh added. He seemed equally upset by Amanda's plan. "They'd shut the whole school down."

"Relax, guys." Amanda smiled calmly and took another sip of the coffee she'd grabbed at the corner delicatessen on the way to school. "I'm not going to print it. But I want people to *think* it's our lead story in the next issue of the *Spectator*."

There was a sharp rap at the door. For a moment, everyone froze.

"Hide that thing, quick!" Amanda ordered Josh, who was still holding the article. He put it behind his back as Pepper called out, "Who is it?"

"Me." The voice was muffled.

"Me who?" Amanda demanded.

"What is this, twenty questions?" the voice outside the door replied. "Either you let me in, or I drop out of school."

"It's Mick!" Josh ran to the door, unlocked it, and threw it open.

"That's Michael Soultaire to you, dude," Mick said, giving Josh a high five as he sauntered past him into the room.

Amanda nearly gasped. He seemed more handsome than ever. The indigo sweater he wore over his pin-striped shirt and regulation school tie gave his eyes a special sparkle. She shook her head in awe. "It's amazing. One minute you're from the streets, and the next you're Super Prep."

Pepper nodded. "Like Dr. Jekyll and Mr. Hyde."

Josh handed Mick the article he was holding. "Take a look at this."

Amanda started to protest, but Josh stopped her. "Mandy, he should see this. He's in on it, too."

"I'm not so sure about that." Amanda put her hands on her hips. "Why'd you disappear last night?"

"I told you. I don't like cops."

Amanda sighed heavily. "They weren't going to arrest you. They just wanted to ask a few questions. What's so terrible about that?"

"I'm sure that among the three of you, all of their questions were answered." As if to close the issue, Mick picked up the article and perched on the edge of the table to read it. When he finished he whistled low. "You sure know how to play hardball."

"I'm not planning to print it. I just want to use it as a decoy to draw out whoever's trying to hurt us."

"You show them something like this, you won't just have your brake line punctured—"

"How'd you know about that?" Amanda interrupted.

"I told him," Josh confessed. "I called the garage and then I called Fleet Street."

"Hold it! Time out!" Pepper put her hands together to form a T. "This conversation has taken a detour and left me back at the main road." She peered over her glasses at the group. "Did I hear someone say my brake line was *punctured*?"

"Didn't the garage tell you?" Josh asked.

"No!" Pepper shouted. She glared at Amanda accusingly. "I don't think anyone's telling me anything!"

Amanda explained, "It appears the crash we had yesterday was not an accident. Josh suspected the brakeline had been punctured so that a slow leak would cause them to fail. The mechanic confirmed it."

Josh said, "It's a main modus operandi—"

"Speak English," Pepper interrupted.

"Uh, murder method," Josh continued. "Used in detective stories. Whenever they want to knock off a rich relative, they fix the brakes."

"I'm not rich!" Pepper shouted. "And I'm barely related to anyone. I mean, there's my mom and dad, but I hardly see *him* anymore."

"Pepper, calm down." Amanda put her hands on her friend's shoulders. "You're starting to babble."

"I always do that when I'm scared out of my wits!" Pepper snapped.

Amanda chuckled. "I know. And that only makes me nervous, so try to calm down, okay?"

Pepper sat down on one of the folding chairs and took several deep breaths. "Okay. I'm calm." She looked up at the others. "I just have one question. When did they do it?"

Josh cleared his throat. "I've been giving it a lot of thought, and I figure it could have been done while you were at school, or while we were all at Groucho's. It only takes a few minutes."

Pepper snapped her fingers. "That blond guy with the tattoo. Remember, the one we saw outside?"

Mick nodded grimly. "I'd say he's a real contender."

"Or it could have been the guy who rammed us," Amanda reminded them. "He was at Groucho's, too."

Pepper collapsed into the green chair by Mr. Mooney's desk. "This is heavy."

Mick checked to make sure the door to the Coop was securely locked. Then he motioned the others to gather around the big metal desk. He leaned on the corner and loosened his tie. "From now on, everyone has to take precautions," he said in a low, intense voice. "It's not just Amanda they're after, it's the entire *Spectator* staff."

Josh pulled up a folding chair and sat next to Pepper. "Jason Stuart, too?"

Pepper shook her head. "They wouldn't go after the Greaseman, he's too single-minded. I mean, the only thing he cares about is getting his story in the paper."

"Which keeps him as a suspect," Amanda said, taking a perch atop the low file cabinet.

"That dork?" Pepper laughed.

"Don't laugh too hard," Amanda cautioned. "Jason's got more raw brain power than anyone in this room. He could easily have cut your brake line, Pepper. And he's clever enough to send notes and make them look like the work of sorority girls."

"What about Mr. Mooney?" Josh wondered. "Do you think he might be in danger?"

"I doubt it," Pepper replied. "Besides, he's never around long enough to get in harm's way."

"I'm beginning to doubt his existence," Mick said, tearing a piece of paper off a legal pad and scribbling a few notes. "I mean, I've been here since Monday and never seen him."

"You just keep missing him," Josh said. "He was here earlier, but he forgot his grade book at home, so he left."

"That guy would forget his head if it weren't glued on," Pepper cracked.

"Don't say that," Amanda cut in. "I like him. Even if he is a little absentminded."

"Okay." Mick looked up from his writing. "I've outlined a plan." He held up the paper. "First, we use the buddy system. Nobody does *anything* alone at school."

The others nodded their agreement.

"Between classes, we meet up in the Hub." He put his hand on Amanda's wrist. "Mandy, don't go to your locker anymore. Who knows what they might put in it."

"Okay." Amanda nodded, terribly aware of the feel of his hand on her arm.

Mick consulted his paper once more. "Now, I think Pepper should show the article to the president of the Gammas, uh . . . what's her name?"

Pepper sat forward. "Bonnie Branch."

"Yeah. Then I'll hit up Whitney Powell—"

"For a date, or information?" Amanda had meant the crack as a joke. Instead it only sounded sarcastic.

Mick looked her straight in the eye. "Maybe both. I'll just wait and see."

Amanda wanted to kick herself. Mick continued, "Amanda, you show it to the other sorority's president."

She nodded. "That's Janis Stevens of Entre Nous." Amanda hoped she sounded cool and confident.

"I doubt if we'll get any big confession out of anybody," Mick said. "But their reactions might give us some clues."

Amanda dug in her pack and handed everyone a copy of the article. "It'll be easier if we each have our own copy."

"Smart." Mick nodded his approval.

"What should I do, Mick?" Josh eagerly leaned forward in his seat.

Mick pointed his pencil at him. "Stick close to Pepper and, if you get a chance, give this guy Stuart the once-over. We want to make sure we cover all our bases."

Amanda tossed her thick, dark hair over her shoulder with a quick shake of her head. "Should you and I team up?" she asked casually.

"Yeah." His lips curled into the barest half-smile. "That is, if you trust me."

The sly gleam in his eye made Amanda's heart race. She hesitated, unsure how to respond. Then the chime signaling the start of the period saved Amanda from having to answer. She picked up her pack and slung it over one shoulder. "We meet back here at lunch."

"That doesn't give us much time," Pepper said, grabbing her books and looping her Nikon around her neck.

"Time enough, if we get a move on," Mick replied, hopping off the desk. "Okay, team—go for it!"

The four of them moved toward the east wing of Sutter with new determination. Pepper spotted Bonnie Branch heading down the hall. "Looks like I'm first. Stay close."

She jogged off to catch up with the Gamma president. "Bonnie, wait up!"

"Pepper, I'm on my way to P.E., " Bonnie replied without breaking stride. "I hate to be late suiting up."

"Listen, I understand," Pepper said, running alongside her. She had to take two steps for every one of Bonnie's. "Can I just show you something really quick?"

Bonnie checked her watch. "Okay. But hurry."

The two girls stopped walking, and Mick and Amanda ducked into the little alcove just outside the gym to eavesdrop. There was a rustling sound as Pepper handed Bonnie the announcement. Then silence.

"What are they doing?" Amanda whispered. "I can't hear a thing."

"I think old Bonnie's reading your article," Mick whispered back. "Give her time."

Bonnie laughed loudly. Little bits of paper fluttered past the alcove as Bonnie stepped into view.

"She'll see us!" Amanda flattened her back against the wall in an effort to hide.

Suddenly Mick leaned one hand against the wall by her head and buried his face in her hair. His back and arms obscured any sight of her from the hallway.

"Close your eyes," he whispered.

Amanda squeezed her eyes shut.

"Now, giggle."

That wasn't hard. His whispering tickled her neck. The hard part was to stop giggling long enough to hear Bonnie's final words.

"You'll never prove this." Bonnie laughed. "Not in a

million years." Amanda opened one eye and watched Bonnie jog to the gym.

"She didn't sound very guilty," Mick murmured into her hair.

"Sometimes the guilty seem the most innocent," Amanda answered without moving a muscle.

"Okay, you two, break it up!"

Amanda sprang out of the alcove, nearly choking herself on Mick's arm.

"Pepper, Bonnie almost saw us," Amanda stammered, groping for an explanation. "We had to act, um . . ."

"Inconspicuous," Mick said with a straight face.

"Yes, that's the word." Amanda nodded vigorously. "Inconspicuous."

Pepper pushed her glasses up on her nose and sniffed, "A likely story."

Josh, who had positioned himself farther down the hall, ran up to them and gasped, "Quick! Whitney's crossing the Hub toward the west wing."

Mick straightened his tie. "My turn."

He pushed his way through the crowd of students clustered around the fountain. Mick caught up with Whitney just as she was stepping into the west wing. "Whitney, mind if I walk you to class?"

Amanda and Pepper followed close behind them, knowing that Whitney would never look back.

Whitney's face lit up with a sparkling smile. "Of course not, Michael," she giggled. "You can walk me anywhere."

"Make me gag," Pepper whispered under her

breath. Amanda nudged her hard with her elbow, then held a math book in front of their faces.

Mick leaned close to Whitney's ear, and soft rumblings, followed by high-pitched giggles, sounded in front of them.

"What's going on up there?" Amanda grumbled.

"I think it's called sweet nothings," Pepper replied, peering over the top of the book.

"Ooh, that makes me mad!" Amanda hissed. "How could he? I mean, with *her*?"

Pepper tilted her head to look in Amanda's face. "Do I detect a note of jealousy?"

"Jealousy! Are you kidding?" Amanda stopped walking. "He's supposed to be getting her reaction to the article, not playing Casanova."

"Do you mean to tell me that Mick's flirting with Miss Whitney Powell means nothing to you at all?"

"He can flirt with whomever he likes. It's a free country."

"Sorry, my mistake," Pepper said. "I guess I thought you were kind of hot on him."

"On Mick?" Amanda stepped back, banging into several students. "I don't even know the guy." Amanda's voice was getting louder and louder. "Whatever gave you that idea?"

"Keep it down, will you?" Josh said, stepping between the two girls. "People can hear you all over west wing."

Amanda glanced around and blinked at her cousin. "Where are Mick and Whitney?"

"They rounded the corner several minutes ago, while you two were arguing."

"Why didn't you tell us?" Pepper and Amanda shouted at Josh. "We could be missing everything."

They scurried down the hall but screeched to a halt just before turning the corner.

"She can't do this!" they heard Whitney shout. "It's a lie, all of it! I'm going to Miss Wilson and put an end to this. Amanda Hart is a menace, and she has to be stopped!"

"That sounds like a threat to me," Pepper murmured beside Amanda. "I think Whitney's our girl."

Amanda peeked around the corner and watched Whitney stomp off down the corridor. "We can't be sure. Everyone knows how easily Whitney loses her temper. She's likely to say anything when she's angry."

The final bell rang, and the halls were suddenly deserted. Mick sauntered over to their group and handed Amanda a crumpled piece of paper. "That's what I call a reaction."

"We heard," Amanda said. "She sounded pretty angry."

"Angry?" he repeated. "Sparks were flying." Mick jokingly patted his clothes and asked, "Do I have any singe marks on me?"

"None that are visible." Amanda responded.

"The final bell has sounded," a math teacher named Mr. Anders called out as he drew the door to his room closed. "You students should be in class." He popped it open again and ordered, *"Now!"*

*   *   *

The next three hours seemed interminable. The four of them met between classes but found no sign of Janis Stevens. Amanda's third period Art History class was one long drone, and when the chime finally sounded she was the first out of the room. But it was lunchtime and she found herself caught up in the wave of students surging outside onto the patio. Amanda drifted along with the flow and was surprised to find herself standing right next to Janis Stevens.

"Finally!" Amanda muttered under her breath. "A lucky break."

Janis turned her head and smiled. "Amanda! I've been trying to find you all morning."

"That's funny," Amanda said, taking a seat beside Janis on the fountain wall. "I've been looking for you, too."

"Wonderful!" Janis set her small gray leather purse on her lap and opened it. The purse matched her shoes, which of course matched her outfit, a soft, gray skirt with a pale pink and gray silk blouse. "Several of us at Entre Nous volunteered to sell tickets to the dance on Friday. I wondered if you were going?"

"Dance?" Amanda had forgotten all about it. It seemed like years since Brad Elliot had mentioned it on Monday. "Gosh, Janis, I—I hadn't thought about it."

"The ticket sales are for a really good cause," Janis said, encouraging her. "The Student Council is giving half to charity, and the other half to the Gammas for their trip to Disneyland."

"The Gammas?" Amanda blinked at Janis. "Somehow I thought that your two clubs didn't like each other."

"Oh, people exaggerate." Janis waved a delicate hand in the air. "That was ages ago, and things have changed."

"I see." This was certainly news to Amanda, but she tried to sound convincing. "I'm glad to hear it."

"I'm chairing the decorating committee for the dance," Janis said. "If you'd like, you could come help us make them tonight." She smiled warmly and added, "We could get to know each other a bit better."

"I'd like that." Amanda realized this might be a good opportunity for her to meet some people outside of the *Spectator* staff. "Maybe I *will* go to the dance."

"Good." Janis tucked a strand of her chin-length blond hair behind one ear. "Now it's your turn." She looked at Amanda expectantly.

Amanda looked up at her in confusion. "Sorry?"

"What was it you wanted to see me about?"

"Oh. This article." Amanda almost felt embarrassed to show it to Janis after she'd been so nice to her. She hesitated for a moment, then handed Janis the piece of paper. "I wrote this last night and thought you should see it before we went to press."

Janis nodded and glanced down at the article. Amanda watched her carefully as she read it from beginning to end. Then Janis read it again. Several times.

Amanda was prepared for her to laugh loudly, like Bonnie Branch, or get really angry, like Whitney Powell. But she was not prepared for what happened next.

CHAPTER ELEVEN

S he cried?" Pepper clapped her hands to her face in obvious shock.

Amanda nodded. "She not only cried, she wept uncontrollably for the entire lunch hour. I mean, I spent most of it with her in the bathroom."

Josh shook his head in amazement. It was the last period of the day, and the three of them sat clustered around Mr. Mooney's desk in the Coop. Amanda had barely waited to get in the door before she had blurted out her news.

"What upset her so much?" Josh asked.

"The truth." Amanda dug into her pack and pulled out her lavender notepad. "I jotted down some notes after I talked to her. It was *too* unreal."

The door to the Coop flew open. It banged against the wall and Pepper screamed.

Mick stood framed in the doorway. He glared at Amanda darkly. "Where were you?"

"What are you so angry about?" she asked, a bit startled by his dramatic behavior.

"Answer my question!" he commanded.

"No." She folded her arms stubbornly. "Not if you're going to behave like that."

Mick stepped into the room and kicked the door shut behind him. "Look, we made a deal," he snapped. "We agreed to use the buddy system. No one was to go anywhere alone. Fine. Great. Then I go to pick you up after your third-period class—and you're not there!"

"It's nothing to get so upset about," Amanda said in a rational tone of voice. "I went to the Hub."

"While I ran all over this damn school looking for you!"

"Look, Mick, I'm sorry I forgot, but you have no reason to get so mad." She shrugged. "I thought I'd give you a little more time with Whitney."

"Not funny!" He took off his jacket and tossed it onto a chair. "What do you think this is, a game?" He pushed up his sleeves and loosened his tie with a quick jerk. The preppie Michael Soultaire was disappearing by the second. "We're not playing around anymore, Miss Debutante." Mick leaned forward, and a lock of his hair fell over one eye. "Apparently, the seriousness of this whole thing has not sunk into your pretty little head."

"More than you know," she shot back. "I met with Janis Stevens at lunch."

"And didn't tell any of us?" He threw his hands in the air and paced the room. "Look, I don't know what you think I'm doing here," he ranted, "but it is not my idea of fun to masquerade as a *geek*." He yanked the school tie off and hurled it against the wall.

"Hey, Mick, chill out," Pepper said.

"How do I drive it into your brain that we are dealing with real threats?" He took a deep breath. "I'd suggest bringing in the cops if I thought we could prove anything."

"The police?" Amanda blinked at him in disbelief.

"Yes." Placing his hands on her shoulders, Mick leaned in close to her face and repeated, "The *cops*." He pulled away abruptly and slumped down on a chair nearby. He looked exhausted.

"I'm sorry, Mandy," Mick said finally, shaking his head, "but you gave me a scare."

"Sorry." This time she meant it. Seeing how upset he was made her feel frightened. "I won't let it happen again."

An awkward silence hung in the room. Finally Pepper broke the tension. "Well. Are we all rational human beings again?"

The two of them nodded.

"Okay, then tell Mick what you found out at lunch, Mandy."

"I showed Janis the article," Amanda said.

Mick nodded. "And?"

"She went to pieces right in front of me." Amanda

looked down at the lavender pad she still clutched in her hand. "She was pretty upset, so it's possible I might have misunderstood some of what she told me. One thing for sure, though, shoplifting is *definitely* going on at Sutter in a major way."

"More than the pledges?" Pepper asked.

"Everyone in Entre Nous."

"Wow!" Pepper sat down at the table, completely dumbfounded.

"And it's not just a pledge prank, either," Mandy added. "Although it started out that way."

"So Heather *was* telling the truth," Josh mused.

"Not quite." Amanda shifted her position on her seat. "Janis wasn't sure when Entre Nous began making their pledges steal something as part of their initiation, but she led me to believe it's been going on for years. Long enough to have become a tradition."

Pepper snorted. "Some tradition."

"The pledges had to steal something small, not worth more than a couple of dollars."

"That gold necklace was worth a lot more than a few bucks," Mick drawled. "When did they decide to go big time?"

"Are you ready for this?" Amanda asked. "When someone started blackmailing them."

"Who?" Mick and Pepper asked at the same time.

"She wouldn't say," Amanda replied. "But Janis said that right after pledge week this fall, someone—she doesn't know who—found out what they were up to and threatened to blow the whistle on the whole sorority if they didn't keep stealing—only now they're forced to steal for him."

"The blackmailer?" Mick asked.

"Right. Janis said she's never seen or talked to him. But every week someone in Entre Nous receives a note—"

Pepper sat forward. "Like the ones you've been getting?"

Amanda nodded. "Blue stationery. Typewritten. Everything's the same. The note gives the poor girl explicit instructions on what to steal and where to drop it off. It's a different location every week."

"You mean, he walks right onto the school grounds whenever he wants to?" Pepper asked with a shudder. "That really gives me the creeps!"

"Everything's starting to fall into place," Josh said. "No wonder the blackmailer tried to get you to kill the story on the sororities."

"He was afraid if you looked too closely, you might uncover his tidy little operation," Pepper added.

Mick held up his hand. "Are you sure she's telling the truth?"

"Almost positive." Amanda tucked her notepad back in her pack. "Look, Janis is an honor student, respected by everyone. She's not exactly the type to want to shoplift."

"Or have to," Pepper said. "I mean, look at her clothes. The girl's already got money."

"Mick, if you had seen how upset she was when I showed her the article, you would have believed her." Amanda shook her head sympathetically. "She looked like she was on the edge of a nervous breakdown. It must be horrible to be trapped in a situation like that."

"Why didn't Janis and the rest of Entre Nous just refuse to steal any more?" Josh asked. "All the books I've ever read say you should never cooperate with a blackmailer."

"It's easier said than done," Mick said darkly.

"They were probably afraid," Amanda added, glancing at Mick. "It would have meant admitting to everyone—the school, their parents, all the other students—that they were a bunch of common thieves. They'd be branded for life."

Pepper nodded. "Yeah, what top college is going to want to admit a confessed thief?"

"Amazing," Josh murmured. "It doesn't seem possible that it could happen at Sutter."

Amanda nodded. "A lot of the girls in Entre Nous come from some of the oldest families in San Francisco. It's hard to believe Janis or Heather is even *capable* of doing something like this."

"Welcome to the real world," Mick said sourly. "People will do anything—steal, blackmail, murder, *anything*—if they're desperate enough."

The room seemed to grow darker with each word he spoke. The cold, hard tone of his voice sent a shiver up Amanda's back.

"That does it." Pepper slammed her hands on the table. "It's time to talk to Miss Wilson. This is really getting out of hand."

"Pepper, wait," Amanda said, putting a hand on her arm. "I promised Janis that I'd keep it a secret."

"Mandy, how could you?"

Amanda shrugged. "She was so upset. She pleaded

with me for a little more time. She insisted that the sorority would put an end to it soon."

Pepper clutched her stomach. "I don't feel good. None of this sounds right."

The phone suddenly rang and everyone jumped.

"I'll get it." Mick said, moving toward the sound of the ring. He stopped and looked around in confusion. "If I can find it." The phone rang again. The sound was emanating from inside the desk.

"Mr. Mooney must have hidden it again," Amanda said. "He thinks that'll keep kids from using it to make long-distance phone calls." She shook her head in amusement. "The trouble is, he always hides it in the same place."

"And when it rings," Pepper added, "it's a dead give-away."

Mick opened the bottom drawer of the green metal desk and picked up the receiver. "Journalism. May I help you?"

Pepper rolled her eyes at his formality on the phone.

"One moment." He covered the receiver with his hand and whispered, "It's for you, Amanda."

Amanda hurried over to the desk. Mick held the receiver up to her ear at an angle, then leaned in close so he could overhear the conversation.

"Amanda Hart?" a muffled voice asked.

"Yes. Who is this?"

"Never mind. If you want to find out who's behind everything, be at 222 Icehouse Alley, seven-thirty tonight."

"Why? What will I find?" Amanda prodded. She was answered by a loud click and then the hum of the dial tone.

"Who was it?" Pepper asked as Mick hung up the receiver and put the phone back in the drawer.

Amanda shook her head uncertainly. "I'm not sure. The voice was muffled, like there was something covering the mouthpiece, but I *think* it sounded like Heather Grey."

"222 Icehouse Alley." Mick scribbled the address on a piece of paper. He tucked the note into his shirt pocket and said, "I know the place."

"Where is it?" Amanda asked.

"Between North Beach and the Embarcadero. An old warehouse district." He looked troubled. "Not a place you'd want to be after dark."

"Well, someone's got to go."

"Amanda, I don't want to go anywhere," Pepper cut in. "This is all really giving me the creeps."

"You don't have to," Amanda replied. "I'm going."

"Whoa, hold it!" Mick said. "Not to that address you're not."

"This thing could drag on and on until someone at the school gets hurt. I say we go, find out who the blackmailer is, and get it over with."

"I think it sounds like a trap," Pepper protested.

"I agree with Pepper," Josh chimed in.

Amanda pushed her hair off her face. "I don't think so."

"How can you be sure?" Josh asked.

"I just have a gut feeling."

"So do I," Pepper groaned. "And it's not good."

"Okay," Mick said suddenly. "You should go. But I'm going with you. I know that part of town."

"We'll take my scooter," Amanda suggested. "I had the tire fixed and have kept it inside the house. No one has tampered with it."

"Yet," Pepper added ominously.

"Then it's settled," Mick said. "Give me your address and I'll be there at seven."

"Why don't you just come with me after school?"

"I've got some things to take care of beforehand." Mick slipped his jacket on and shoved his tie into his pocket. "Josh, you walk them home," he ordered, "and *don't* let them out of your sight."

"Got it!" Josh saluted.

Mick threw open the door and cocked his finger at Amanda. "Seven?"

Amanda nodded. "Seven."

Mick started to leave, then stuck his head back in the room. "Oh, and wear something black."

"Black?" Amanda tilted her head.

"Yeah. To blend into the night." As he strolled out of the room, he murmured, "Besides, I have a feeling you look dynamite in black."

The door swung shut behind him, leaving a stunned Amanda.

"This sounds more like a date than a stakeout," Pepper said.

"Oh, Pepper, get real." Amanda didn't want to admit that she thought so, too. She was already mentally ransacking her closet for something to wear. Something black.

CHAPTER TWELVE

A t three minutes to seven Amanda stepped in front of the full-length mirror hanging in the entryway and examined her outfit critically. For the past hour she had been trying on clothes and was feeling a little silly about it. She'd taken more time choosing this night's outfit than she'd spent picking a dress for the prom the year before. After trying on every dark-colored thing she had in her closet, Amanda had finally settled on a pair of stonewashed jeans, a thick wool turtleneck, and her brushed-suede jacket for warmth. All in black, of course. She'd brushed her dark hair until it fell perfectly, thick and full around her shoulders.

Amanda took a deep breath and stared hard at her own reflection. It was the same face she had been looking at for sixteen years. The high cheekbones and aquiline nose she'd gotten from her mother. Her green eyes, framed by dark eyelashes and eyebrows, came from her father. But there was something new in the face that stared back at her, a special intensity that made her features seem more sharp-edged.

Is it nervousness? she asked herself. *Or just plain fear?* The doorbell rang and she jumped at the sound.

Mick was leaning easily against the sill when she threw open the door. He took one look at her face and asked, "Scared?"

He had seen it, too. Amanda nodded. "Mostly because I'm not sure what lies ahead." She picked up two helmets from the chair by the door and handed him one. They stepped out onto the porch, where her purple scooter sat waiting. "How about you?"

"Yeah, I'm nervous. I'd be stupid not to be." Slipping the helmet over his head, Mick took the scooter from her and carried it down the steps to the street.

He started to get on the scooter first, but Amanda stopped him. "I may be scared, but not too scared to drive my own scooter."

Mick opened his mouth to say something, then shrugged. "Suit yourself." He stepped away from the scooter and made a deep bow. "After you."

"Thank you," Amanda replied graciously. She fastened her helmet, then hopped onto the front seat and turned on the ignition.

Mick looped his leg over the seat behind her. "I was right."

"About what?" she asked, revving the engine.

Mick leaned forward and whispered, "Black's definitely your color."

Amanda smiled and released the clutch. As they sped off down the road, Mick wrapped his strong arms around her waist and leaned with her into the curve. Her eyes closed for the briefest of seconds as a pleasant surge of exhilaration came over her. *Better keep your mind on the road,* she thought.

Mick shouted instructions, guiding them toward their rendezvous. Soon the tidy houses of North Beach gave way to the sleazy strip joints and seedy bars that made this part of San Francisco so notorious.

The sidewalks were crowded with people spilling out onto the street, making it difficult for her to maneuver safely. The noise was deafening. Horns were honking, and pounding music blared from the neon-rimmed entrances to the nightclubs. Taxi drivers leaned out of their windows, cursing at groups of jaywalking sailors. Worst of all were the garishly dressed barkers haranguing passersby to come inside.

She kept her eyes glued straight ahead and tried to ignore their crude shouts. Mick's arms tightened around her waist as they pulled up to the stoplight.

"You doing okay?" Mick murmured into her ear.

Amanda nodded gratefully. Just the sound of his deep voice reassured her jangled nerves. Then a huge black man, clad in a wide-brimmed hat and white silk suit, loomed in front of her, blocking the way. Several gold earrings dangled from his left ear, and a matching gold tooth gleamed from his mouth as his face creased in a smile.

"It's my man, Mickey Soul!"

"Sylvester! Hey, dude!"

Amanda couldn't believe her ears. Mick knew this guy?

The man called Sylvester gave Amanda an appraising look and murmured, "My, my, but we are a beautiful sight!" He turned back to Mick. "Good to see you, little brother."

The light turned green and Mick shouted, "Later!" as they drew away from the crowded intersection and headed down Broadway.

"Who was that?" Amanda shouted over the rush of the wind in their faces.

"Sylvester," Mick replied. "Don't worry, he's a friend."

"Really?" Amanda tried to keep the doubt out of her voice and sound confident. What did she *really* know about Mickey Soul? He worked for a bicycle messenger service. He had access to some nice clothes, he was clever, and he seemed to know his way around the unsavory side of San Francisco. But as to where he lived, how old he was, where he went to school (if he even *went* to school), she had no idea.

Right then she felt a little frightened of the dark-haired stranger whose arms were wrapped tightly around her waist.

"Pull in here." The sound of his voice in her ear startled her. Amanda flicked on the turn signal and guided the scooter into what looked like a black tunnel. Fire escapes lined the sides of the old brick buildings, and garbage cans sat in clusters along the cobblestoned alley. She slowed the scooter, swerving to avoid puddles of water as they bounced over the bumpy surface.

"Stop here," Mick hissed. Amanda put on the brake and Mick whispered, "What time is it?"

She checked her watch. "Seven twenty-three."

"Not much time." Mick got off the scooter and looked around him. He pointed to a doorway that was blocked by several trash cans. "We'll hide over here."

Amanda wheeled the scooter into the little doorsill. The garbage smelled awful, and she held her breath as she passed it. Luckily there was a wooden crate behind the cans, so she didn't have to kneel on the ground.

"What do we do now?" she whispered as the two of them crouched in the dark corner.

"We wait."

Amanda shivered and pulled her jacket close around her. Every nerve in her body was tuned to the sounds of the alley.

Suddenly Mick clutched her arm and pointed. Two figures emerged out of the darkness. From their hiding place they had a clear shot of a girl. She was wearing a light trench coat and carried a package wrapped in brown paper. She looked both ways to make sure no one was watching, then carefully placed the package in a cardboard carton and slid it behind the dark green dumpster. The girl pulled her coat tight around her, then joined her friend and hurried down the alley.

Amanda leaped up to follow, but Mick grabbed her by the arm. "Wait. Let's see what happens."

"I think we should find out who the girls are," Amanda whispered breathlessly.

Mick suddenly put his hand over her mouth. "Listen."

Her heart pounded in her ears. Then she heard them. More footsteps. Soft, padded ones. *Must be wearing sneakers,* she thought. Mick eased the pressure of his hand over her mouth and gestured toward the dumpster. The running had stopped. She stared hard through their peekhole. Suddenly there was a flash of movement as a figure darted behind the dumpster. He scooped up the parcel, and Amanda gasped.

"It's the blond guy from Groucho's! Look at his tattoo."

"I see it," Mick answered grimly.

They watched him kick the carton back behind the dumpster and run.

"Follow him," Amanda urged.

"And leave you here alone? Are you nuts?"

"It's our only chance to find out who he is." Amanda sprang to her feet. "Go!"

Mick hesitated and she said, "I'm going to check out the girls."

"No, you stay right here," he ordered. "I'll only be a few minutes. You'll be safe if you just stay put. Promise?"

"Okay, but hurry! He's getting away."

Mick leaped lightly over the top of the garbage cans and vanished into the shadows. Amanda closed her eyes and listened to the sound of his footsteps fade

away down the alley. When she opened them, everything seemed to have intensified.

The night was deathly still. The garbage smelled
rotten. A breeze rattled the rusted fire escapes, and
Amanda jumped back against the wall. Visions of rats
and awful bugs crawling everywhere filled her mind.
Her throat grew tight with panic. She knew she had to
get out of there.

Amanda stumbled to her scooter. She didn't care if
Mick came back or not. She was going to go home.
Home to a nice, warm bedroom, with strong locks on
the door. She'd be safe there. She would cancel the
articles and write her parents, asking if she could join
them overseas.

The gravel crunched behind her. "Mick?" She spun
to face him. "I was starting to get scared . . ."

Her voice trailed off as she realized that Mick wasn't
there. Amanda strained to see into the darkness. Suddenly she gasped with fright. Someone else was with
her in the alley—so close that Amanda could hear
breathing. Her body went rigid and she mechanically
put her leg over the seat of her scooter. *Please let me
get this started. Please!* Amanda fumbled in her
pocket for the key, and the gravel crunched again.
This time it was nearer.

Where's the key? her mind screamed. She groped
desperately for it in her pocket and finally felt the cool
metal in her hand. *One more second, and I'm safe.*
Her whole arm shook as she aimed for the ignition.

A strong blow sent her head crashing down on the handlebars. Searing pain arched through her skull, and a blinding light filled the alley. Then everything went black.

CHAPTER THIRTEEN

A manda opened her eyes and quickly shut them again. The room swirled around her in a blur of color and light. She let her mind clear, then stared up at the ceiling and forced her eyes to focus.

Above her head a strip of neon light flickered against the flat gray wall. A pipe with peeling paint ran across the top of the ceiling. She moved her hand slightly and felt a canvaslike texture beneath her fingers. *I'm lying on some kind of cot,* she thought. *But where am I?*

Amanda tried to turn her head to the side, and a sharp pain shot through the back of her skull. Then she turned her head again and almost cried out in fright.

Only inches from her cheek was a face from a nightmare. Two intense black eyes watched her closely. She realized she'd seen the face before. But where? Amanda stared back unblinkingly, trying to remember.

"I think she's waking up," the man called over his shoulder. The movement drew his face out of the deep shadows and revealed the pockmarks scarring his face.

It was the guy in the green Pontiac! She wanted to scream but couldn't find her voice.

Her mind was racing, absorbing every detail about the room. It seemed to be a storeroom of some kind. Cardboard boxes were stacked carelessly against the walls. A few wooden crates had been placed around a beat-up old card table, with a telephone and an answering machine resting on it.

Oh, no! I've been kidnapped, she thought. *I'm being held for ransom. They're waiting for a call from my aunt and uncle, and then they'll probably kill me.* Amanda turned her head and groaned. *All for a stupid article about sororities.*

The curtain over the door rustled. A short, chubby man with a gray moustache came into the room. He had a white towel draped over his forearm and two packages of frozen vegetables in his hand. He knelt beside Amanda and, wrapping the frozen food in the towel, gently pressed them against her forehead.

"How do you feel, *chica?*" he asked. "You've got one nasty bump on your head."

Before Amanda could reply the curtains parted

again and Mick stood framed in the doorsill. She nearly fainted in shock. *Of course!* she thought, *now it all makes sense. He's the mastermind behind this whole kidnapping scheme.*

Amanda pushed the towel off her head and made a move to jump off the cot. The room did cartwheels and she wobbled dangerously.

"Whoa, wait a minute!" Mick sprang forward and caught her before she fell. He guided her gently back onto the cot. "You're not going anywhere. Not in your condition."

Amanda finally found her voice. "How could you!" she said, tears springing to her eyes. "I trusted you. And so did Josh and Pepper!"

"What are you talking about?" Mick knelt in front of her as she sat up on the cot. With one hand he smoothed her hair back from her face. "Mandy, someone knocked you out cold in the alley. Gabe brought you here."

"Where's here?"

"Fleet Street." Mick grinned his lopsided grin. "Which is actually the back of Emilio's Corner Grocery. He's Gabe's father."

Amanda's eyes suddenly widened, and she leaned forward to whisper in Mick's ear, "Gabe's the one with the green car."

Mick whispered back conspiratorially, "I know."

"No, you don't understand." Amanda felt like her mind was full of cobwebs. She grabbed the collar of his jacket and whispered more intensely. "Mickey, he was at Groucho's. Then he rammed Pepper's car, trying to kill us. And I think he's the one who hit me."

Mick looked at her for a moment in stunned silence. Then he threw back his head and laughed. Amanda pushed him away angrily, and he fell back onto the concrete floor.

"It's not funny!" she snapped.

"But it is," Mick said, getting to his feet. He chuckled and rubbed his chin. "Gabe has been helping me keep an eye on you."

"What?" Amanda stared in disbelief at the stocky boy with the tough face.

"He's also my best friend," Mick added. He gestured for him to step forward. "Gabriel Sanchez, meet Amanda Hart."

"I feel like I already know you," Gabe said, his face creasing into a warm smile. Suddenly he didn't seem so intimidating.

"I told Gabe to meet us in the alley," Mick explained. "But he got there too late."

Gabe winced. "Sorry about that. Boy, did you give me a scare."

"Me, too," Mick agreed. "I wanted to kick myself for leaving you alone." He studied her face. "Should we take you to the hospital? How are you feeling?"

"I think I'm okay," Amanda said, trying to absorb all of the new information. She took a deep breath. "I just have a headache."

Emilio picked up the towel and frozen foods and

said, "Here, put this back on your head. You'll feel better."

She did as she was told. He patted her on the shoulder, then said to Gabe and Mick, "I've got to get back to the store. Let me know if she needs anything."

"I'll be fine, Mr. Sanchez," Amanda said. "Thank you for everything." He smiled and left the room. As soon as he was gone, Amanda turned to Mick and asked, "What did you find out?"

"Plenty." Mick sat beside her on the cot. "I followed the guy with the tattoo—"

"To his house?" she interrupted.

"No. He headed for a pawnshop on Howard Street. Sold the goods pretty fast. Then he delivered the money to his boss."

"You mean he's not the leader?" Amanda leaned forward. "Then who is? Someone from a street gang?"

"No." Mick folded his hands in front of him and looked at her uneasily. "It's someone at Sutter."

"*What?*"

"It's an inside job."

"Wait. How do you know that?"

"The payoff was made in the parking lot at the school. I couldn't get close enough to see who was there. When they got the money, they went back inside the building."

"But it's nighttime. What were people doing at the school?"

Mick shrugged. "I don't know, but the gym was all lit up and there were still cars in the parking lot."

"Oh, that's right—the dance." She nodded. "They're

probably making decorations for Fall Fest on Friday night." She pressed her fingers to her temples. Her head was starting to throb again.

Mick stood up and faced her. "As I see it, someone at Sutter is blackmailing Entre Nous and trying to make it look like it's coming from outside."

"Oh, boy, this is too much! I need to go home and think." Amanda stood up and wobbled on her feet. She still felt a little woozy. "Home!" she gasped. "What time is it? How long have I been here? My aunt and uncle are going to be worried sick."

"Relax." Mick slipped one arm around her waist to steady her. "It's almost ten, but don't worry. I called Josh and explained everything. He said he'd handle your relatives." His eyes filled with concern. "I'll take you home now. You've had a rough one, kid."

Mick led her out the back door to where her scooter was parked and called, "Gabe, hold the fort."

"No sweat, buddy," Gabe replied and turned to go back inside.

"Gabe, wait!" Amanda said. "I—I want to thank you for helping in all of this. I hope I didn't seem too rude inside."

"*De nada*. It's nothing," he replied with a wave of his hand. "Just don't go into any more dark alleys, okay?"

Amanda grinned and started to get on the front of the scooter.

"Hold it!" Mick caught her before she was completely seated. "This time I'm driving. I don't care if it *is* your bike."

Amanda was too tired to argue. She slid back on the seat, and Mick started the engine. Moments later they were riding toward the Marina. Amanda closed her eyes and wrapped her arms tightly around Mick's waist. She suddenly felt incredibly tired. She lay her head on his shoulder. As they rode along, she could feel the muscles in his back shift. For the first time that night she felt warm and safe again.

"You doing okay?" he called over his shoulder, as they waited for the light to change at an intersection.

"Umm," Amanda murmured drowsily. "I feel just fine."

CHAPTER FOURTEEN

A manda called an emergency meeting the next morning in the Coop. With Mick's help, she explained to Pepper and Josh what had happened the night before.

"I knew that guy with the tattoo had to be in on it," Pepper said, pounding the table. "I didn't like his eyes. They were too beady."

"But who could be his boss?" Josh asked. "I can't believe anyone at Sutter is that devious."

Pepper shrugged. "I think the question is, who needs the money badly enough to blackmail an entire sorority?"

"And try to hurt anyone who got in the way," Amanda added ominously.

"Jason Stuart needs the money," Josh pointed out. "To get into Stanford."

"True," Pepper agreed. "And he has made it pretty clear how he feels about sororities."

"What about the Gammas?" Amanda asked. "For the past two months all they've talked about is needing money. They might blackmail Entre Nous to get it."

"I know the two sororities have never liked each other," Pepper said, "but would they go to all that trouble for a trip to Disneyland?"

Amanda pursed her lips. "That wouldn't make sense."

Mick folded his arms and announced to the group, "My money's on Whitney Powell." He shook his head in disgust. "That girl *never* has any cash. I've seen her in action. She has guys buy her everything."

"Yeah, Whitney is a leech." Pepper took off her glasses and polished them on her shirt. "But I doubt if she would be hitting people in dark alleys just to have more pocket money."

Amanda shrugged. "That's the trouble with all of this. None of these people seem to have a strong enough motive."

"What about Heather Grey?" Josh spoke up in his quiet voice. "She's the one who set you up to get knocked on the head."

"I said I *thought* it sounded like Heather on the phone," Amanda stressed. "But I could never be certain. Besides, I think she wanted us to see what was going on and help put a stop to it."

Pepper slid her wire-rim glasses back up onto her nose. "I bet she'll be as happy as we are to see this thing over and done with."

"If she was trying to help solve the mystery," Josh said, turning a paperweight over and over in his hand, "why would she just drop out of the academy?"

"What!" Amanda and Pepper said in unison. "When?"

"When I was in the office yesterday helping one of the counselors with her computer, I overheard Miss Wilson tell Mr. Wolfe that Heather had withdrawn."

Amanda shook her head. "Heather must really be scared."

"Yeah," Mick grumbled. "Scared that we're getting too close. So she dropped out of school and arranged to have you beat up in the alley." He crossed his arms in front of him. "I'm putting Heather at the top of my list."

Amanda sat down on one of the tall stools. "Boy, she seems so nice."

"Don't let appearances fool you," Mick said. "Whoever is behind this has some sort of screw loose."

Pepper shrugged. "I'd say whoever's behind it is really clever."

"Clever!" Mick repeated. "To involve so many people in a blackmailing scheme, and then try to waste anyone who finds out about it?" Mick shook his head. "That person's cheese has definitely slipped off her cracker."

Amanda started to giggle but winced in pain. She

put her hand up to her head and felt the huge lump beneath her thick, dark hair.

"Still hurt?" Mick asked, watching her with concern in his eyes.

She nodded. "But only when I laugh."

"I'm just glad you're alive," Pepper said. "When Josh called and told me what had happened, I nearly died of fright. And that was just hearing about it. I can imagine what I would have done if I'd been there."

"The same thing I did," Amanda said. "Pass out."

"Yeah," Mick agreed soberly. "You should count yourself lucky that you did."

"You know, guys," Pepper said in a low voice, "this is really getting out of our league. I think we should call the police."

"I'm with Pepper," Josh said. "I didn't tell my parents about what happened last night because you asked me not to. But what if it had been worse?"

Mick threw his hands up in the air. "What kind of evidence do we have? Mandy's been hit over the head in a dark alley." He laughed bitterly. "You tell the cops that, and they'll say it serves her right for going down there."

"Mick's right," Amanda said, looking at the group. "We know that the blackmailer goes to Sutter. I think we're getting close to finding out who it is. The police would just confuse the issue. Besides . . ." She shrugged. "Who's better equipped to find out what's happening here than us?"

"Well, if we're going to play detective," Pepper said

sarcastically, "we'd better have a plan. Anybody have any bright ideas?"

"Yes." Amanda dug in her pack and pulled out her leather-bound notebook. "After I got home last night, I came up with an idea." She consulted her notes. "Tomorrow night is the Fall Fest. All of our suspects should be there."

"Suspects?" Pepper raised an eyebrow. "You're sounding more and more like a detective by the second."

Amanda smiled at her friend. "We not only have to sound like detectives, we have to think like them. The way I figure it is, we lay low for the rest of today and act like nothing happened."

"And then?" Pepper asked.

"Then tomorrow night—we force their hand at the dance."

"Great idea," Mick said. "But how?"

Amanda flipped the page of her notebook. "We spread the word that I know who's behind the blackmailing and that I plan to make an announcement at ten o'clock in front of the entire dance."

"No, Mandy!" Pepper exclaimed. "You might as well wear a target on your chest. What are you trying to do?"

"Get this thing over with," Amanda replied. "Once and for all. Besides, no one is going to try anything in a crowd. They'll try to get me alone."

"Which will be impossible," Mick said. "Because I'm going to stick to you like glue."

Amanda felt her pulse quicken. "You mean, we'll go together?"

"Uh . . . no." Mick jammed his hands in his pockets and stared at the floor. "Whitney's asked me to go with her."

"Whitney!" Amanda's cheeks suddenly felt hot with embarrassment. "I thought she was broke."

"I did, too, but she seems to have gotten some money from somewhere. She even offered to buy me dinner."

"Well, I hope you two will be very happy together. Just remember, while you are out having a good time," Amanda said, biting off each word tartly, "the rest of us will be risking our lives trying to solve this case."

"Whoa, wait a minute." Mick turned to Pepper. "Has she always had that temper?"

Pepper nodded emphatically. "Always."

"Thanks, Pepper," Amanda muttered.

Mick peered into her face. "Mandy, the only reason I took this date with Miss Powell is because she looks like our number-one suspect."

Amanda shrugged her shoulders.

"And I don't want to have her running around loose, hitting you on the head."

Amanda stared hard into his blue eyes to see if he was telling the truth. She hoped he was. "Well, now that you mention it, Brad Elliot asked me to the dance. I should see if the invitation is still open."

"You have a date?" Mick's eyes widened. "Well, that's, uh . . . great." Suddenly his voice changed.

"Wait a minute, who is this Brad guy? Can we trust him?"

"In the back seat of a Trans Am?" Pepper cut in. "No."

Amanda shot her a warning look and Pepper said, "But as a dancing partner in a crowded room, no problem."

Before Mick could protest, Pepper clapped her hands together. "Well! Now that we've got you two dates, who am I going to go with?"

Amanda smiled. "You and Josh could go together."

"As the Odd Couple," Pepper cracked, then turned to Josh. "No offense, kid, but I *am* almost three years older than you."

Josh's ears turned a bright pink and he mumbled, "That's all right. Besides, I can't dance. I was planning to spend tomorrow night working on the computer system and finishing the paper."

"So what am I going to do?" Pepper demanded.

"I've got it," Mick said, snapping his fingers. "I think Pepper should go with Gabe."

"Gabe?" Pepper lifted a skeptical eyebrow. "Who's Gabe? I don't remember meeting anybody named Gabe."

Mick took Pepper by the elbow and led her to the window. He raised the shade and gestured toward the alley. "That's Gabe."

Gabe was leaning against the door of his green Pontiac, a wrench in one hand and an oily rag in the other.

To all appearances he looked like an amateur mechanic hard at work on his car.

Pepper lifted her Nikon camera to one eye and focused the telephoto lens on the dark-haired boy. "I remember him!" she gasped. "From Groucho's and the accident. He looks so mean!"

Amanda put a reassuring hand on her friend's arm. "Pepper, he's not. He's Mick's best friend."

Mick opened the window and let out a loud whistle. Gabe bobbed his head up at the sound, and Mick motioned for him to come onto the school grounds.

"What are you doing, Mick?" Pepper cried, clutching his arm. "I can't go with him. He really does look scary."

"Gabe is about the gentlest person I know," Mick said, smiling at his friend. "Unless you cross him. And if someone even *thought* about hurting a friend of Gabe's . . ." Mick raised his eyebrows meaningfully. "Well, I wouldn't want to clean up the mess."

"That settles it," Amanda said. "You're going with Gabe."

Pepper watched the hulking fellow jog up the steps toward the Coop and echoed in a tiny little voice, "I'm going with Gabe."

CHAPTER FIFTEEN

L ucky for you, my date got sick," Brad Elliot said as he ushered Amanda to his car on Friday night. "Do you usually call guys at the last minute to ask them out?"

Amanda wanted to say, "Only when I'm desperate." But she bit her tongue and replied sweetly, "Not usually. But we decided that the *Spectator* needed a reporter at the dance, and I remembered your invitation from Monday. You don't mind, do you?"

"Mind?" Brad threw open the door to his maroon BMW. "I think it's great." He leaned forward and wiggled his eyebrows. "By the way, black looks outstanding on you."

Amanda blushed. Mick had said the same thing. She wondered if that had been the reason she'd chosen the black cashmere minidress. It was cut in a low vee in the back that showed off her trim shoulders. The sweater dress clung to the curves of her figure, and she'd pulled her hair to the side with a black bow. Amanda usually avoided heels because of her height and because the hilly streets of San Francisco made walking in them sheer agony. But tonight she'd slipped on a pair of black brushed-suede pumps that showed off her long legs. Just before leaving the house, she spritzed an extra dash of her new perfume, Reminiscence, behind one ear. Mick had been right. The fragrance smelled delicious.

She slid into the front seat of Brad's car and shivered with anticipation. So much could happen in the next few hours. Brad flicked on the radio and beat his hand on the dashboard in time to the music. Amanda was relieved they wouldn't have to make small talk.

She heard a low rumbling, and the dim headlights of a large car drew close behind them. Amanda watched, casually at first, wondering why it made such a loud sound. Then she noticed that whenever they turned, the car followed. A sideways glance at Brad told her that he hadn't noticed that they were being tailed. He was too busy bobbing his head in time to the music.

"Brad?" she asked casually, "when was the last time you checked your brake fluid?"

He turned down the radio and stared at her. "I don't think I heard you right. Were you asking about my brakes?"

"Yes." She smiled pleasantly. "I was just thinking

that living in a hilly city like this, you must have to have your brakes checked a lot."

"Well, as a matter of fact, I just had the car worked on." He looked at her oddly. "It's funny you should ask because it was touch and go whether they'd have it ready in time to pick you up."

Amanda sank back in her seat with a sigh of relief. "I'm really glad to hear that."

"That I almost didn't make it tonight?" Brad looked more mystified by the moment.

"No, no!" Amanda said quickly. "It's just nice to know that you take such good care of your car." She added flatteringly, "It's such a *great* car."

He smiled smugly and patted the dashboard. "Yeah, she's hot, isn't she?"

"Sure is." Amanda glanced in the rearview mirror and watched as the rumbling car behind them got closer and closer. Suddenly she sat bolt upright in her seat.

Two figures were silhouetted in the windshield. The curly-topped head with the outline of glasses was unmistakable, as was the dark menacing posture of the driver.

"Pepper and Gabe!" she whispered under her breath. They'd been following her ever since she left her aunt and uncle's house. *I should have recognized the loud muffler,* she thought with a smile. *About as subtle as a Mack truck.*

They reached the school, and Brad parked the car in the student lot. Music blared from the direction of the Sutter gymnasium. Amanda watched as Gabe cut the lights on his green Pontiac and parked a short distance away. Gabe, sporting a white dinner jacket and black pants, hopped out and scurried to open Pepper's door. He had to kick it several times. Finally it opened with a loud screech and Pepper stepped out.

"Charming," she announced sarcastically.

Pepper wore a strapless satin dress that she had borrowed from Amanda. The deep midnight-blue really showed off her red hair. If it weren't for the ever-present camera and light meter dangling from her neck, Pepper would have looked quite elegant.

Brad offered Amanda his arm, and they joined Pepper and Gabe in the front foyer of the gym. Couples stood clustered in little groups chatting. Through the main doors, Amanda could see the outlines of people dancing. Spotlights circled the crowd, pausing just long enough to feature different couples as they danced.

Brad nodded at several passersby and then called over the music, "Hey, Pepper, you look hot!" Brad nudged Amanda. "That's a good one. Hot Pepper! Get it?"

Amanda rolled her eyes and chuckled. "I got it, Brad."

"Will you excuse me for a moment, Amanda?" Brad gestured to the far side of the room. "I need to check on the refreshments. Student Council is in charge."

As he dove into the crush of people, Amanda called out, "But, Brad, our tickets!"

"At the front table," he shouted. "Just pick them up." Then he disappeared onto the dance floor.

Amanda turned to Pepper and Gabe. "Well, I guess things could be worse. He could be hanging onto me every minute."

Amanda led them to the table by the entrance to the gym. "Two tickets under the name of Brad Elliot," she said to the girl sitting with the cash box. The girl opened a little tin box that held the tickets and shuffled through the pile.

Janis Stevens, in a green velvet bolero jacket and matching skirt, appeared behind the ticket taker. A beautiful cameo was pinned to the throat of her high-necked lace blouse. "Mandy, I'm glad you could make it. You know, we missed you at the decorating."

"Oh, I'm sorry, Janis, I couldn't come. Something . . . came up." Amanda tucked her tickets into her small black purse. "How's the turnout?"

"Fabulous!" Janis gestured to the crowded gym. "This is even bigger than Homecoming last year."

Pepper raised her camera to one eye and snapped Janis's picture. "The Gammas should make a bundle on this, right?"

For the briefest moment, a dark cloud crossed Janis's face. Then she smiled brightly. "That's right. We're all very excited for them."

One of the pledges caught Janis's attention and she moved back into the dance. "I'll talk to you later."

"She looks like she stepped out of a Laura Ashley catalog," Pepper said as they watched Janis walk away.

Amanda nodded and sighed. "Janis always looks like a porcelain doll. Almost as if she'd break if you touched her."

Gabe peeked into the huge gym and shook his head slowly. "Man, the band is smokin'." He laughed to himself. "My school never threw anything like this!"

Pepper shrugged. "It's just a dance with a few decorations in a gym. So what?"

"My school's idea of a gym is cracked asphalt surrounded by a chain-link fence," Gabe cracked. "A dance usually means a gang fight."

Amanda's ears perked up. At last, a chance to find out about Mick Soul's *real* life! "Do you and Mick go to school together?"

Before Gabe could answer, Pepper cut in. "Warning! The Greaseman is rolling our way." She raised her camera and flashed it directly in Jason's face.

"Cut it out, Pepper," Jason Stuart grumbled, blinking. "Are you trying to blind me?"

"No, I just wanted to preserve this moment for posterity. You, in a dinner jacket. Without your briefcase."

Jason shot her a scathing look, then said, "Amanda, I'd like you to meet my date, Kimberly Irvin."

Amanda realized he was holding the hand of a short plump girl with wispy blond hair. She looked vaguely familiar. "You're a freshman, right?"

Kimberly nodded shyly. Jason put his arm around the girl's shoulder and announced, "Kimberly helped me with my award-winning science project."

"I didn't really work on it," Kimberly protested weakly. "I just helped out a little."

"Well, you certainly helped me demonstrate it at

the state Science Fair." Jason beamed at Amanda.
"She was even with me at the awards ceremony."

"Where was that?" Amanda asked.

"Sacramento, on Wednesday night. They gave me
this ribbon." He put one thumb under his lapel and
stuck out his chest. A huge blue ribbon reading "All-
State Champion" hung from his lapel. Amanda was
surprised she hadn't noticed it before.

"Well, congratulations, Jason, that should really im-
press the scholarship committee at Stanford." Amanda
shook his hand as she thought, *If he was in Sacramento Wednesday, no way could he have been in that
alley.*

"It's too bad the *Spectator* photographer wasn't
there to capture the event." Jason gave Pepper a sour
look. "It was an important moment for the school."

"Well, it's never too late." Pepper raised the camera
to one eye and the flash went off again, capturing
Jason's scowl. "It should be a good one."

Jason looked at Amanda. "How do you put up with
her?"

"It's difficult." Amanda sighed dramatically. "But
somehow I manage."

The music changed to a loud pounding rhythm.
"This is one of my favorite songs," Jason exclaimed. He
grabbed Kimberly by the hand. "Let's go dance."

The two of them gallumphed toward the dance
floor. "I've never seen two people more perfect for
each other," Pepper cracked. "Tweedledee, meet
Tweedledum."

"One thing for sure, Jason's in the clear," Amanda said as she watched him jumping up and down on the dance floor. "There's no way he could have been in two places at once."

"It's a pity, too." Pepper sighed. "Of all the suspects, I kind of hoped it was him. He's such a squid."

Gabe had been standing beside them, quietly checking out the crowd around them. Suddenly his face broke into a wide grin. "Yo, dude!"

Amanda turned to see who Gabe was calling to, and her heart leaped into her throat. Mick Soul stood just inside the foyer. With one hand in his jacket pocket, he coolly surveyed the gathering. He was wearing a classic double-breasted tuxedo, with gleaming black patent leather shoes, a wing collar with a hand-knotted bow tie, and French cuffs that peeked out a perfect quarter-inch below his sleeves. A simple white rosebud was pinned to the satin lapel. He looked as if he'd just stepped out of a movie from the thirties.

Some people were born to wear evening clothes, Amanda thought with a smile. *And Mickey Soul is definitely one of them.*

"Mick—I mean, Michael!" Gabe waved a hand. "Over here."

Mick nodded in his direction, then turned back to the door. He held out his hand, and Whitney made her entrance. She paused just inside the door to make sure everyone noticed her arrival. Little beams of light danced over her sequined bodice. An amber sash separated it from the skirt that billowed out like a ballet dancer's chiffon skirt around her legs. She looked spectacularly beautiful, and Amanda suddenly felt very drab by comparison.

Pepper took several pictures, then lowered her camera and whistled softly. "They look like a million bucks."

"Yeah," Amanda muttered. "But whose million?"

The crowd parted, allowing the dazzling couple to pass through them into the gym. Mick put his arm on Whitney's elbow, and Amanda felt a tight knot form in her chest. She put on her prettiest smile to make the feeling disappear.

Mick spotted Amanda, and his eyes took in her whole appearance at a glance. His lips parted into a pleased half-smile and he murmured softly, "Oh, yes!"

A surge of warmth raced through Amanda's veins. But her pleasure was short-lived.

"Oh, Amanda, I didn't expect to see you here," Whitney said, looping her arm through Mick's. "Are you working the door or something?"

"No, Whitney," Amanda replied, looking directly at her. "I have a date."

"Date?" Whitney's eyes widened in exaggerated shock. "What a surprise."

"We're awfully catty tonight, aren't we," Pepper said between clenched teeth.

"Speak for yourself," Whitney shot back.

"And your outfit," Pepper went on. "It's so rad. How could you ever afford it?"

Amanda stepped closer to hear Whitney's answer.

"Maybe I won the lottery," Whitney said sweetly.

Then she put her face right into Amanda's. "Or maybe I stole it. Put *that* in your little newspaper!"

Amanda backed away, a little shocked by the vehemence of Whitney's attack. She couldn't think of anything to say.

"Come on, Michael, let's go find some people I like," Whitney urged in her pouty voice.

Mick ushered her toward the door to the gym. He turned and mouthed over his shoulder, "Later."

"I think Whitney's our blackmailer," Pepper whispered. "Gotta be."

Brad reappeared. His jacket was off and he had a small stain on the front of his tux shirt. "Amanda, I'm sorry about this, but they delivered the wrong refreshments. We wanted Coke, and someone brought Gatorade. Twenty cases of it. I had to make a call to the local store to get some Coke sent over *pronto*."

"Remind me to just hit the water fountain," Pepper mumbled as she and Gabe made their way into the dance.

Brad put his black jacket back on and asked, "Did you pick up the tickets?"

"Got them right here." Amanda fumbled for the little white envelope in her purse. "I almost forgot."

She opened the envelope and pulled out two tickets. A pale blue piece of paper was clipped to the back of one of them. She recognized the stationery. Just the sight of it made her feel as if a cold hand had seized her heart. Amanda handed Brad his ticket and turned slightly to shield the note from his view. She took a deep breath and unfolded the slip of paper.

Her knees went weak. She lost her balance and stumbled sideways into Brad. As she tried to steady herself, she crammed the note back into her purse.

"Are you okay?" Brad peered into her face anxiously. "You look like you've seen a ghost."

She may as well have. The words scrawled on the note floated in big, angry letters before her eyes:

SAY GOODBYE, AMANDA.

CHAPTER SIXTEEN

M|inutes later Amanda was finally able to get Mick, Pepper, and Gabe all in one corner of the gym. They huddled by the edge of the bandstand and she showed them the note.

"Good!" Mick said as he handed it back to Amanda. "Our plan is working."

"How can you say that?" Pepper hissed. "That note reads very much like a death threat to me."

"To me too." Mick nodded seriously, then turned to Amanda and said, "Which is why I'm not letting you out of my sight."

Amanda was starting to get very jumpy. "Oh, yeah? Then why was it so hard for me to pry you away from Whitney?"

Mick winced. "Sorry about that. She can be very—uh, persuasive."

"I bet she can," Amanda snapped.

An exuberant dancer on the floor bumped into Amanda hard. She let out a frightened squeal and leaped forward into Mick's arms.

"Relax, Mandy, stay cool," he whispered softly into her ear. "You need all of your wits about you if you're going to be able to spot danger when it's near."

"Everything is starting to feel dangerous," she answered.

"I'm right here," he assured her. "And so is Gabe. We won't let anything happen to you." He looked into her eyes and grinned. "Come on, give me a smile. We're going to nail this creep tonight, once and for all. Remember that."

Amanda nodded and stepped away from him. She straightened her dress, trying to regain her composure. "I'm sorry. Maybe I should get a glass of Gatorade, or something gross like that."

"Maybe we all should," Mick replied jovially. He turned and looked around for Whitney. She was standing about twenty feet away, talking to some friends from her sorority.

"Whitney," Mick called, "I'm going to get my cousin something to drink."

"Okay," she replied, "but don't be long." She turned back to her friends and their gossip. "Can you believe that sack Stacy Pendleton's got on?" Amanda heard

Whitney say. "Where'd she get it, San Francisco Tent and Awning?"

Brad was standing by the open back door of the gym, having a heated discussion with a deliveryman. "I really don't see why we should pay for your mistake," Brad was saying.

"Brad!" Amanda caught his eye and made a drinking motion with her hand. He nodded distractedly and turned back to his argument. Amanda joined the others as they plunged into the crowd of dancers and headed for the refreshment tables.

Halfway across the floor Amanda saw something that made her knees lock with fright. She stood frozen, surrounded by jostling bodies dancing to the music. "Mick!" she whispered hoarsely.

"What?" He put his face close to hers to hear.

"That blond guy from the alley. He's here!"

Amanda pointed to a tall figure moving through the crowd. He smoothed his stringy blond hair back off his forehead and she spotted the tattoo covering his hand.

"You don't think he's someone's date, do you?" Mick wondered.

"He'd have to be," Amanda answered. "You're required to have a student I.D. to buy the tickets. Sutter Academy is very strict about that."

"Hey, if you're not gonna dance, get off the floor," a guy who bumped into them called good-naturedly. "I need some elbow room."

The band switched to a slow ballad, and before Amanda could leave Mick spun her into his arms. "I know we're here on business," he said softly, "but I couldn't let a whole evening go by without dancing at least one dance with you."

Mick wrapped his arms snugly around her waist. They were dancing so close she could feel the music of the band through their bodies. "Where's the guy with the tattoo?" Mick asked, spinning them in a circle.

Amanda scanned the crowd. "He's standing over by the bandstand."

"Let's check him out." Mick led her expertly along the perimeter of the gym floor, weaving smoothly in and out of the other couples.

Amanda was truly amazed at his fluid movement. Usually when she danced with a guy, she had to worry about what move they would make next and whether she would step on his feet. With Mick, dancing was effortless. All she had to do was relax and he made her look good. "Where'd you learn to dance like that?"

"I worked for Arthur Murray one summer."

"You're kidding!" Amanda pulled her head back to look at him. She never could really tell if he was teasing her.

"Am I?" He spun her away from him, then drew her back in. Then, with a rapid series of turns and some nimble footwork, they arrived at the edge of the bandstand, only feet away from where the blond guy had been standing.

Amanda's eyes were shining. "I'm impressed."

"So am I," Bonnie Branch declared from beside them. She was dancing with Terry Mann, the star forward on Sutter's basketball team.

"Hey, Michael, you'll have to show me your moves," Terry cracked. "Maybe I can use them on the court."

Mick flashed a big smile. "Anytime."

The music switched to a fast number and the couples danced apart.

"I noticed the paper didn't make it out this week," Bonnie said. "I didn't think Miss Wilson would let you print that lie."

"It's not a lie," Amanda said. "And I'm going to be naming the person behind it all at ten o'clock."

Bonnie's eyes widened for a second. Then she checked her watch. "That's a half-hour from now."

"Half an hour!" Amanda repeated. She caught Mick's eye. This could be embarrassing. She'd promised to reveal a name at ten o'clock, and she still hadn't a clue. As far as she was concerned, everyone seemed guilty.

Bonnie grabbed Terry's arm. "I'm thirsty."

Terry nodded, and the two of them turned to leave.

"What are we going to do?" Amanda asked desperately. Mick started to answer, then stopped as Brad appeared beside them.

"Hey, what is this?" he said. "I turn my back for one second and you're off dancing with another guy." He nodded brusquely at Mick. "No offense, Soultaire, but she is my date, you know."

Mick held up his hands in mock innocence. "She's my cousin—we used to dance together when we were growing up."

"I thought you were going to get something to drink," Brad said to Amanda.

"I was," she replied. "But we never made it to the refreshment stand. Boy, am I thirsty."

"Here, have a sip of my soda. We finally got it straightened out." Brad held out his drink, and his arm jerked in the air. Ice cubes and cola exploded into the air.

Amanda tried to leap out of the way, but Mick was behind her. The cola splattered across her chest and dripped down the front of her cashmere dress.

"Boy, Amanda, I'm sorry," Brad said, pulling a handkerchief out of his pocket and offering it to her. "Someone bumped my arm. I hope your dress isn't ruined."

Amanda tried to dab at the stain, but it was useless. "I'd better go to wash this off."

Brad nodded. "I'll get some paper towels and clean the floor."

As she turned to leave, Mick clutched her arm. "Be careful," he warned in her ear. Then in a lighter tone, he said, "I'll be keeping an eye on the beautiful scenery." He winked at Brad as a pretty redhead walked by.

Amanda shook her head, then made her way toward the ladies' room. It was at the far end of the gym, by the locker rooms. The soda on her neck and hands had begun to dry and felt sticky and awful. She pushed open the door and headed straight for the sink. Amanda turned on the faucet, tore a paper towel from the dispenser, and glanced in the mirror.

"Oh!" She jumped, then laughed nervously. "I didn't see you there."

Janis Stevens leaned against the wall behind her. Her ivory skin was red and blotchy, and dark smudges of mascara were underneath her eyes. It was clear she had been crying.

"I didn't mean to scare you." Janis sniffled. "It's just that I'm so upset."

Janis covered her face with her hands and slid down the tiled wall to the floor. She sat in a heap, sobbing.

Amanda knelt beside her. "Janis, tell me what's the matter."

"That guy," Janis whimpered. "He's here."

"What guy?" Amanda could feel her pulse start to race. "The one who's blackmailing you?"

Janis nodded miserably.

"The one with the tattoo?" Amanda prodded gently.

Janis answered with a choked sob. "He gave me this note." She held up her right hand. A sheet of blue stationery was crumpled in her fingers. It was horribly familiar to Amanda.

"May I read it?" Amanda asked.

Janis wasn't listening. She clutched the paper to her chest, her eyes wide with fear. "Now he says he needs more money and there's no end in sight." She struggled to stand up. "I can't take this pressure anymore. I don't care if they do throw me in jail for stealing, I'm calling the police."

Amanda moved to the sink. She carefully folded a paper towel and held it under the cold water faucet. *We have to call the police. There's no turning back now*, she thought. The tattooed guy was in the gym.

Janis could identify him as her blackmailer and had the note to prove it. The police probably could make him talk, and then the entire nightmare would be over.

"Here, put this on your forehead," she urged, returning to Janis's side. "You'll feel better."

"What should we do now?" Janis asked, dabbing her eyes with the paper towel.

"Call the police. We should have done it a week ago."

They moved toward the bathroom door, Janis still clutching the note to her chest. "There's a pay phone in the foyer," Amanda said, reaching for the door.

"No!" Janis drew back in terror. "I can't go back out there with all those people. Someone might hear."

"It's the only phone in the gym."

"There has to be another phone." A large shiny tear rolled down one cheek. "Don't you have one in the Journalism building?"

"You're right," Amanda admitted. "I always forget about it because Mr. Mooney keeps it hidden in his desk."

"Let's use that one," Janis pleaded. "We could exit by the side door, and no one would see me."

Amanda hesitated for only a second. She'd promised Mick not to take any chances. *But this really isn't a chance*, she told herself. *I'll just unlock the building, and Janis can make her call. I'll be back at the dance before Mick even notices I'm gone.*

"Do you have a key?" Janis asked.

Amanda nodded. "Mr. Mooney gave me one because he's always losing his. Now, don't worry, Janis, everything's going to be fine." She opened the bathroom door and peered out into the gym. Most of the students were gathered around the bandstand. The exit door was only about ten feet away. If they hurried, no one would see them, and they'd be safe. "Okay," she whispered. "Let's run for it."

She threw open the swinging door and made a beeline for the exit. Pushing on the metal handle, Amanda hurried out the door and down the landscaped hill toward the Coop. Janis followed in silence. At the door, Amanda peered nervously over her shoulder, then felt in her little black bag for her keys.

The moment she opened the door, she could sense that something was wrong. The same musty smell hit her in the face, but a new, unfamiliar scent was mingled with it. Almost like cologne. She stepped inside and spotted a small green glow coming from near the far wall.

"Josh's computer! It's on." Amanda backed up and whispered, "Janis, let's go back to the dance. Something's not right in here."

"I can't go back there," Janis whimpered. "Please, let me make the call. And then I'll feel better."

Amanda felt the wall to the right of the door and flicked on the light switch. The room was bare. Nothing seemed out of the ordinary except Josh's computer. Could he have been so absentminded that he forgot to turn it off that day at school?

Absentminded. Of course. Mr. Mooney must have been using it. Or trying to use it. It would be just like him to forget to turn it off.

"It's in the bottom drawer of the desk," Amanda said under her breath. "You make the call. I'll keep watch." She stood in the doorway and watched Janis cross to the desk and open the drawer. She pulled out the phone and set her crumpled note on the desk.

"I can't dial, Mandy!" Janis held out her hand. It was shaking violently. "I'm too upset. Please, do it for me."

"Okay." Amanda stepped into the room and moved to the desk. "But you stand guard."

As she picked up the receiver and propped it against her ear, she glanced at the note lying beside the phone. The sheet of paper was blank! She flattened it out and turned it over. There wasn't a word written on it.

Amanda's eyes widened. Janis had lied about the note in the bathroom to lure Amanda away from the dance. *Why?* Amanda felt like she'd been hit in the stomach as she realized only one person could have access to that blue stationery—the blackmailer.

Her knees turned to gelatin. She willed her legs not to buckle. *If I can just dial 911, everything will be fine.*

There was a rustle of movement behind her. She felt a bony hand clamp down over her mouth.

"I'd put that back down," a male voice said. "Nice and easy."

She twisted her neck to get a look at her captor. All she could see was the tattoo of a snake coiling around his hand.

Janis walked in front of Amanda and stared at her coldly. She was completely transformed. "Everything would have been just fine if you hadn't interfered."

Amanda tried to scream, but the sound was muffled by his grip over her mouth. His nails dug into her face and she felt a sharp pain in her arm as he twisted it behind her.

"You know, we could have been friends," Janis said, carefully unplugging the phone cord. "But you can't say I didn't warn you."

"Quit the talking," the blond guy grumbled. "Let's get this over with."

He took Amanda by the shoulder and threw her against the wall next to the closet. The impact knocked the wind out of her, and she fell heavily to the ground. The collision made the closet door swing open slowly.

"Josh!" Amanda gasped. Her cousin lay crumpled up among the stacks of newsprint. He was gagged with masking tape across his mouth. As he struggled furiously to break the knots binding his hands and feet, they locked eyes for a moment.

Suddenly Josh focused on something behind her, and his eyes widened in horror. She turned and saw the blond guy wrapping the phone cord around his hands.

"No!" she screamed and lunged toward the door. But he was too quick for her. He looped the cord around her neck and pulled it tight, pressing her close against him. She struggled desperately, gasping for air.

"Do it!" Janis screamed angrily. "Do it now!"

He pulled the cord taut and whispered, "Lights out."

CHAPTER SEVENTEEN

The room began to spin. Black spots danced in front of Amanda's eyes. She was kicking and fighting for her life when something exploded behind her. The door to the Coop hit the wall, sending bits of plaster crumbling to the floor.

Mick and Gabe leaped into the room. Mick wrapped his arm around her assailant's throat, and Gabe held a tire iron in front of his face.

"Let her go," Mick growled, "or you won't see tomorrow."

The thug loosened his grip, and Amanda fell forward onto the floor, gasping for air. Janis backed slowly out the door. Amanda saw her and rasped, "Stop her!"

Pepper was coming up the walk just as Janis turned to run. She swung her camera at the fleeing girl. It caught Janis behind the knees, and she stumbled and fell to the ground. In a flash Pepper was on top of her, holding her down.

Mick yanked the tattooed guy's jacket down, pinning his arms to his sides. Gabe grabbed an extension cord, whipped it around his ankles and slammed him against the wall.

Mick knelt down beside Amanda. "Are you okay?"

She felt her throat. An ugly, red welt circled it. "I could be better." She coughed hoarsely and asked, "How did you know I was here?"

"When you didn't come back from the bathroom, I sent Pepper in to find you."

Pepper came through the door, pulling Janis behind her. "I saw the blond guy with the tattoo and pointed him out to Gabe."

"We saw him leave the dance and followed him," Mick continued.

They heard a muffled groan coming from the closet. "Oh, my God!" Amanda gasped. "Josh is still in there."

The door had been kicked shut in the struggle. Mick opened the door and removed the gag from Josh's mouth. As soon as it was off, Josh shouted, "Janis is the leader! Don't let her get away!"

"We've got her," Amanda said, kneeling beside him.

"Did you find out who he is?" Josh whispered, gesturing toward the tattooed guy.

"He's Eddie LaFon, otherwise known as the Snake," Mick explained. "Gabe recognized him at the dance. He's got a criminal record as long as your arm."

"You got nothin' on me, turkey," Eddie LaFon hissed.

"Be quiet," Janis ordered. "This is all your fault." Janis turned to the group, her eyes filling with tears. "Eddie caught me shoplifting and made me do this. He's awful. I never wanted to hurt you, ever. Mandy, you're my friend."

This time Amanda wasn't fooled. "Save your tears, Janis, for someone else. I learned my lesson."

"But you've got to believe me," Janis tried to wrestle free of Pepper's grasp. "Please make Pepper stop hurting me."

"You stop trying to run away," Pepper said sweetly, "and I'll stop hurting you."

"Why?" Amanda cocked her head to look at Janis. "Why would a smart, pretty girl like you steal?"

Janis stared at the floor. "I needed the money."

"Shut up!" Eddie snarled. "They've got no proof you've stolen anything."

Amanda felt her neck. "I may not have proof of that, but I'd say three witnesses and this welt are proof enough for attempted murder."

"I had nothing to do with that!" Janis shrieked.

"You did, too," Eddie said quickly. "Remember? We were at the dance and saw a light out here. You thought someone was robbing the school."

Janis's eyes brightened. "That's right."

Amanda shook her head. "I'd say that Eddie's story has a few holes in it. And you were clumsy enough to leave some big clues lying around." Amanda pointed to the crumpled blue stationery. "I wonder what the authorities will think when they find your fingerprints on this? My notes were written on the exact same paper."

Janis's lower lip quivered. "Mandy, what are you going to do now?"

"What you suggested I do before."

"What's that?"

"Call the police." Amanda, knowing how Mick felt about cops, looked in his direction. He gave her a nod, and she plugged in the phone and dialed.

"Josh," Mick said, "you don't mind trading places with these two, do you?"

"It would be a pleasure." Josh held open the closet door, and Gabe shoved Janis and Eddie inside, then leaned against it.

"It's dark in here," Janis whimpered. "I can't breathe."

"Tell me about it," Josh answered. "Try spending an hour in that place."

"You were in there for an hour?" Pepper gasped.

"What were you doing here, anyway?" Amanda asked, as she hung up the phone.

"I was going to work on the computer at home, but I forgot the disk at the Coop," Josh explained. "I wanted to finish so we could get the stuff to the printer's tomorrow."

"Noble," Pepper cracked.

"I was looking through the school's files, trying to reconstruct an article, when I accidentally accessed the student records. I found some *very* interesting things there."

"You found something on Janis, didn't you?" Amanda asked.

Josh pointed across the room at the glowing screen. "It's all there in green and white."

Amanda went to read the screen. Janis's file was there. At first nothing seemed remarkable. But on closer examination, things looked strange. "I didn't know Janis had moved."

"What?" Pepper asked. "I didn't, either. I thought she still lived at the Stratton mansion on Nob Hill."

The mansion was famous for being one of the most elegant in the city. It had survived the San Francisco earthquake of 1905 and was on the historic homes tour every year. The Stevenses were very proud of that fact.

"Now it looks like her address is an apartment in Daly City."

"That's quite a comedown," Mick said.

"Look." Amanda pointed to the bottom of the screen. "Janis applied for financial assistance in September, but recently withdrew the request."

"It doesn't make sense," Pepper said. "Her dad is one of the richest men in San Francisco."

"Who's her dad?" Mick asked.

"Ryland Stevens."

Mick nodded knowingly. "Ryland Stevens *was* one of the richest men in San Francisco. He lost everything in the market crash of '87, including his wife's money."

"How do *you* know all that?" Amanda asked.

Mick shrugged. "I'm a bike messenger. We catch all the dirt in the financial district."

Gabe suddenly held up one hand. "Listen."

Pepper cocked her head. "The band is hot. Too bad we missed most of the dance."

"No." Gabe shook his head. "That other sound."

Finally Amanda heard it, too. The distant wail of sirens. She was certain they were coming to Sutter. Amanda opened the door of the Coop and hurried out to meet the police.

Two squad cars pulled into the parking lot with a squeal of brakes. "Down here!" Amanda and Josh shouted.

Pepper searched the grass for her camera. "I want to catch this on film. I hope this thing still works."

Amanda raced back to the Coop. "Mick, they're here. And there are four of . . ." Her voice trailed off as she looked around the room. The big metal desk had been pushed in front of the closet. The window was open, and a breeze ruffled the papers on the bulletin board.

"He's gone," she murmured in a tiny voice. It was at that moment that the events of the evening suddenly caught up with her. Her throat grew tight, and two huge tears traveled down her cheeks. "And he didn't even say good-bye."

CHAPTER EIGHTEEN

L ater that night, a taxi pulled into the parking lot of Sutter Academy, and three exhausted people climbed into the backseat.

"1414 Chestnut Street, please," Amanda called to the driver. The cab pulled out of the deserted parking lot and roared up the hill.

"Boy, that was some ordeal," Pepper said, taking off her glasses and rubbing her eyes.

"I've never seen so many crying girls." Josh shook his head in amazement.

"Once one girl from Entre Nous confessed to shoplifting, it set off a chain reaction. Twenty-five girls pleading guilty." Pepper slipped her glasses back on. "That was an amazing sight."

Josh folded his arms across his chest. "I still can't get

over Janis Stevens' being the mastermind behind a shoplifting ring."

Amanda took a deep breath and leaned her head back against the seat of the cab. "I've been thinking about it all evening. I think it had a lot to do with something she said last Friday in the Hub."

Pepper cocked her head. "You mean about the sororities and traditions?"

Amanda nodded. "Janis said her great-grandmother, grandmother, and mother were all in Entre Nous. Carrying on tradition and the family name are big—or I guess I should say *were* big in her family."

"It's true," Pepper agreed. "I've always thought of the Stevens family as part of the royalty of San Francisco. You know, riding in limos and entertaining important people. Wintering in the city and summering in France. Shopping trips, parties . . ." She sighed. "A whole other world."

"Can you imagine how hard it must have been for her family to give that up?" Amanda asked. "I guess Janis just couldn't take the humiliation of it all."

"So she decided to pretend it never happened," Pepper said, "and that's why she started shoplifting."

Amanda nodded. "Just to keep up the appearance that her family was still on top."

"Then Eddie caught her and tried to blackmail her," Pepper continued.

"But—" Amanda raised one eyebrow. "Janis was smart. She convinced him to become her partner. She'd supply the shoplifters and he'd be the fence."

"But what I don't understand," Josh said, "is why all the other girls in Entre Nous would shoplift."

"To get into the club," Amanda replied. "It really was an initiation prank."

"Then Janis pretended that someone else had found out," Pepper said, "and was going to turn them in if they didn't keep shoplifting."

"Fear kept them stealing," Amanda concluded. "I think the girls are relieved to be able to finally reveal their awful secret."

"You're probably right." Pepper scratched her chin. "I wonder what will happen to them?"

Amanda pushed her hair back from her forehead. "I think the police understand that they're all basically nice girls who were misled by one pretty sad individual."

They shuddered, thinking how close the evening had come to ending in tragedy.

The cab pulled up to the curb in front of the Pickering house, and they all climbed out. "I think Mom's still up," Josh said, seeing the light glowing from the library. "She'll want to know how the dance went."

"We'll be there in a minute, Josh." Amanda and Pepper sat on the top step of the porch. They stared at the lights of the city around them. The streetlamps were little globes of blurred light as the San Francisco fog rolled in.

"Thinking about Mick?" Pepper asked softly.

Amanda rested her chin on her hands and sighed. "He just vanished."

Pepper smiled. "He's a magician, that guy."

"The least he could have done was say good-bye."
Her eyes started to fill with tears.

"Did you hear that?" Pepper asked suddenly.

Amanda nodded. Someone was whistling. They
peered into the darkness, straining to see who it was.
Suddenly a figure burst out of the fog on his bike.

Gone was the elegant tuxedo and suave figure of
Michael Soultaire. A streetwise boy in a worn leather
jacket and faded jeans had taken his place.

Pepper and Amanda applauded as Mick rolled past
with his entire body stretched across the handlebars
and seat, casually leaning on one elbow.

"Mick!" Amanda cried with delight. "We were afraid
you'd gone forever." Then just as quickly she put her
hands on her hips. "Why did you and Gabe just leave
like that?"

Mick hopped off his bike, catching the seat with one
hand. "I told you—"

"You don't like cops," Amanda finished for him. "I
remember."

Mick grinned his half-smile, and a shock of black
hair fell over one eye. "Right."

"Well, you missed all of the excitement," Amanda
said. "Half the school confessed to shoplifting, crazed
parents arrived to drag their children home—"

"And Miss Wilson could only stand in the foyer
wringing her hands." Pepper imitated the headmistress. "Oh, dear. Oh, dear. This is most unfortu-
nate."

Mick chuckled. "I'll call her on Monday and withdraw from school."

"Do you have to?" Amanda heard herself ask.

Mick shrugged. "The case is closed, and Gabe fixed my bike. I've got to get back to work." His eyes met Amanda's in a steady gaze. "I think I'm going to miss it. Not the school part, but . . ." He paused for a long moment. "Everything else."

There was another long silence.

"Boy, am I tired!" Pepper stretched her arms wide in an exaggerated yawn. "Listen, Mandy, I'm going to go to bed."

"Fine," Amanda said quietly. "I'll be up in a minute."

"Does the entire newspaper staff live here?" Mick asked.

"No," Amanda chuckled. "Pepper's just staying the night."

"We figured we should rehash everything that happened," Pepper cracked. "For our memoirs."

Mick laughed, and Pepper stuck out her hand. "It was fun."

He clasped her hand firmly. "Same here. See ya, Pepper."

"Well, Mick," Amanda said, after Pepper had gone inside, "will I see you again?" She tried to make the question sound casual, but the answer meant a lot to her.

"It's hard to say." Mick studied her face intently. "Your world and mine don't mix too well. I mean, it's a long way from Nob Hill to South Market Street."

Amanda tried to hide the disappointment in her eyes.

Mick hopped on his bike. "But listen, if you ever need me, you know where to call."

Amanda nodded. "Fleet Street."

She held out her hand to shake his. Mick took it and gently pulled her toward him. His lips touched her cheek in a soft kiss, and he whispered into her ear, "Catch you later, Hart."

Amanda watched him ride down the street and disappear into the fog. Her hand touched her face where his lips had brushed her cheek.

"So long, Soul."

CHAPTER NINETEEN

O n Monday, Amanda met Pepper in the Hub before school and handed her the latest issue of the *Sutter Spectator.* "Here it is! Hot off the presses."

"We made it!" Pepper said as she took the newspaper and perched on the edge of the fountain.

Amanda smiled. "And only a week late."

Pepper flipped through the paper. "Where's the sorority story?"

"I killed it." Amanda sat next to Pepper and added, "Too many people have been hurt by Janis Stevens. I didn't want to rub it in."

Pepper nodded. "Wise move."

"Besides," Amanda said cheerfully, "this is much nicer news." She pointed to the headline that read, "Whitney Wins!"

"I can't believe that girl really won the lottery." Pepper shook her head. "Twenty thousand dollars! It's just not fair."

"But she can't touch a penny of it," Amanda said. "Her parents made her put it in a trust fund until she's twenty-one."

Pepper threw back her head and laughed. "Maybe there *is* justice in the world."

Amanda started giggling, and the two friends laughed so hard that tears streamed down their faces. Pepper abruptly stopped and held the newspaper in front of her face. "Warning. Warning. Greasemen at fifty paces."

Amanda wiped her eyes and watched Jason Stuart roll across the Hub. He was clutching a briefcase in one hand and had at least twenty copies of the *Spectator* tucked under his other arm.

"Nice picture, Jason," Pepper said, pointing to the blurred snapshot on page two. "Who took it?"

"My girlfriend, Kimberly," he said, deliberately not looking at Pepper. "We felt the article needed it."

"It needed something," Pepper muttered under her breath.

Amanda nudged Pepper and then smiled pleasantly at Jason. "Well, I hope it helps you get that scholarship to Stanford."

Jason shrugged. "It doesn't really matter. Over the weekend, I decided to go to UCLA." As he waddled off toward the west wing, he called back over his shoulder, "They have a much better science program."

"Hold me back!" Amanda gasped. "All of that fuss

for nothing. I'll strangle him. I'll have him dissected and enter him in the next Science Fair."

Pepper wasn't listening. She had focused all of her attention on the tiny notice on the back page.

"What's this?" She cocked her head to look at Amanda.

Amanda felt her cheeks suddenly heat up. "Oh, that." She tried to sound casual. "We had some extra space and I thought I'd throw that in." She'd lain awake late Friday night, debating whether or not she should run it.

Pepper raised an eyebrow. "Oh?"

"I thought I should do something. I mean, he did save my life."

Pepper read the notice out loud:

One from the Hart
Dark-haired girl with a flair for writing seeks dark-haired boy with a knack for adventure. Purpose: To thank him for everything.

"Do you think he'll ever see this?" Pepper asked, laying the paper in her lap.

"Who knows?" Amanda smiled. "With Mick, anything's possible."

Across the parking lot, a figure dressed in black leaned casually against the gates of Sutter Academy reading a newspaper. He brushed back the lock of hair that had fallen over one eye and turned to the back page. A slow smile crept across his lips. He folded the newspaper and carefully tucked it in his back pocket. As he looped his leg over the seat of his bicycle, the sun caught the shiny spokes of his wheels. In a flash of silver he was gone.

ABOUT THE AUTHOR

JAHNNA N. MALCOLM is really the pen name for a husband and wife team, Jahnna Beecham and Malcolm Hillgartner. Together they have written twenty-one books, including five titles for Bantam's Sweet Dreams series under the name Jahnna Beecham. They are also the authors of a middle-grade series called Bad News Ballet. Both are professional actors and have trod the boards in theatres across the United States and Europe. In fact, they met in an audition and were married on the stage. Jahnna and Malcolm live in Montana with their brand-new baby Dashiell and two old dogs.